W9-BYA-714

CL

CL

A Kiss in the Dark

A Kiss in the Dark

Joan Smith

Thorndike Press • Chivers, Press
Thorndike, Maine USA   Bath, England

This Large Print edition is published by Thorndike Press, USA and by Chivers Press, England.

Published in 1998 in the U.S. by arrangement with The Ballantine Publishing Group, a division of Random House, Inc.

Published in 1998 in the U.K. by arrangement with Ballantine Books.

U.S. Hardcover   0-7862-1352-3   (Candlelight Series Edition)
U.K. Hardcover   0-7540-3224-8   (Chivers Large Print)
U.K. Softcover   0-7540-3225-6   (Camden Large Print)

The text of this Large Print edition is unabridged.
Other aspects of the book may vary from the original edition.

Set in 16 pt. Plantin.

Printed in the United States on permanent paper.

British Library Cataloguing in Publication Data available

Library of Congress Cataloging in Publication Data

Smith, Joan, 1938–
    A kiss in the dark / Joan Smith.
      p. (large print) cm.
    ISBN 0-7862-1352-3 (lg. print : hc : alk. paper)
    1. Large type books. I. Title.
  [PR9199.3.S55157K56   1998]
  813′.54—dc21
                                       97-47178

A Kiss in the Dark

Chapter One

Cressida Charmsworth, Baroness deCourcy to her many acquaintances, Sid to her intimates (she would not tolerate the nickname Cress; it sounded like an aquatic plant), came dashing through the park of Dauntry Castle in her high-perch phaeton. Lord Dauntry, impatiently awaiting her arrival within, caught a glimpse of her rig as it bolted along, taking the curving sweep of road at a precarious fifteen miles an hour. He watched as, with a practiced pull on the reins of her perfectly matched grays, she slowed their pace, finally calling "Whoa!" as she reached her destination. The team danced to a stop, shook their manes, and uttered a well-bred neigh.

Only then did Lady deCourcy look at the castle before her. The honey-colored brick of its long facade glowed in the sunlight of the June afternoon. From the roofline a dozen statues stared haughtily off into space. At the center was a dome, surmounted by a balustrade. Very impressive, but too French to please her. She preferred the English

Gothic style of Tanglewood, her own estate in Kent.

Tanglewood, like the title, was inherited, not acquired through marriage. Her late papa's title and estate descended by heirs general to his daughter, as he had no son. In the normal way the baroness would have spent summer at Tanglewood, but it had become necessary to releat the roof and do some minor repairs to the inside of the house as well. She preferred to be elsewhere while the racket of crowbars and hammers disturbed the tranquillity of home. She had decided to use the occasion to look into the desirability of buying a summer place on the sea.

Brighton had been her first stop. Too crowded! How could one rest and recuperate from the trials of the Season with half of London there, continuing the round of gaieties? Then, too, the duke was there, and he had become very pressing in his advances. The Duke of Sommers had not actually made an offer, so she could not refuse him and be done with it. Eligible though His Grace was, Lady deCourcy was not yet ready to give up her delightful independence.

Since the ripe age of sixteen years, she had been a slave to her invalid papa. She sometimes thought she would die there at Tanglewood, where she had been born and reared. But life had a few surprises in store for her. Upon her papa's death, she discovered that he had been nothing else but a miser, carefully squirreling away his gold while they lived a life of frugality. After her year of mourning, free of encumbrances and as green as grass, she had gone off to London to taste those pleasures so long denied her.

She insisted that at twenty-three she was too old to be eligible. Society responded that with Tanglewood, two thousand acres, and ten thousand a year besides, she was too eligible to be called old. Her mirror told her she was by no means hagged. Her raven hair was unstreaked with silver, her green eyes undimmed, and her cheeks as full and soft as rose petals. None of this was in her mind as she accepted her groom's assistance from the seat of her high-perch phaeton, however. She was merely eager to meet her hostess and landlady, the dowager marchioness of Dauntry, and be shown to her cottage.

As soon as word was out that the baroness wanted to try a summer by the sea, invitations had poured in. She had scanned them all, but in the end had decided to escape the hordes by renting a small house not too far removed from Tanglewood. While returning from an outing on the duke's yacht one afternoon, she had espied a simple wooden Swiss-style cottage *orné* with painted shutters, which seemed to be growing out of the cliff just west of Beachy Head, and decided that was where she wished to spend her summer. Investigation revealed that it was a part of Lord Dauntry's estate. Within the week and without even writing to the marchioness, the baroness had magically received an invitation from the dowager, inviting her to spend the summer at Dauntry Castle. An exchange of letters had settled the misunderstanding. The baroness preferred peace and quiet. She thanked Lady Dauntry for her kind offer, but wished only to rent the cottage on the sea.

After a long look around her, Cressida proceeded up the three broad steps and lifted the lion's-head knocker. The door was opened at once by a model butler who had obviously been awaiting her arrival.

"Your ladyship," he said, bowing punctiliously. "Her ladyship is awaiting you in the Green Saloon."

The baroness was shown into a chamber of impressive dimensions and lavish furnishings. She paid little heed to the Persian carpets, the paintings, and carved furnishings; she was more interested in her hostess. Lady Dauntry, known thus far to Lady deCourcy only through letters, proved to be a plump, matronly lady with gray hair and blue eyes, wearing a plain round gown and a lace cap.

"Do come in, Lady deCourcy," the dame said. "You must be fagged to death after your trip. So wearing, being jostled along in a coach. You will want to freshen up."

"How lovely of you to have me, ma'am," the baroness replied with a smile and a curtsy. "But I am not in the least fagged. It is such a fine day and the trip so short that I drove my phaeton. My companion, Miss Wantage, and my cousin, Mr. Montgomery, are following with the traveling carriage and our mounts. I made it in just over two hours. My grays are admirably trained. The head groom at Chevely — the stud farm at Newmarket, you know — trained them as a favor to me. I could not have done better myself," she said with no notion of puffing herself off. The stables at Tanglewood had been her major entertainment for years.

"You are too modest, ma'am," Lord Dauntry said with a pinch of his nostrils and a lift of his black brow that belied the compliment.

Her eyes slid to Lord Dauntry, who had arisen upon her entrance. He bowed stiffly. The baroness curtsied again. Lord Dauntry was a part of her reason for not wanting to

11

stay at the castle. She had nothing in particular against him, but she was not in the mood for another courting. She assumed that her invitation to the castle had been preferred with that in mind, which was strange, for Dauntry had never dangled after her in London. In fact, she had a distinct impression that he disliked her, despite their being virtual strangers.

She knew he was an extremely eligible member of the Whig aristocracy. His character was unblemished. He was called handsome. Cressida found him less handsome than distinguished. His tall frame was well formed and his face agreeable, although more swarthy and rugged than she liked. Above a pair of cool gray eyes a black slash of brows rose, lending him an angry look that was seldom softened by a smile.

He showed her to a chair of thronelike grandeur.

"It will be so nice to have a young lady here for the summer," Lady Dauntry said, and rambled on, leaving little time for replies. "My daughter, Tony — really Antonia, but we call her Tony — has just married, you must know. How I miss her, and she gone only three days! She and her husband — no doubt you know Lord Harold Quincy, Lord Thorpe's son, with an excellent estate, and close to home too, but they will be away all summer. The Lake District they have gone to for their honeymoon. Have you ever been there, Lady deCourcy?"

"Yes, last autumn. It is charming."

"I have never seen it. Algie has been there, have you not, Algie?"

Lord Dauntry nodded, and the deluge of words rolled on. "Yes, of course you have. My wits are gone begging. I believe it was you who put it in their heads, with your talk of fells and turbulent skies and all those lakes and posts. Harold will like that. The lakes, I mean, not the poetry. He is a great fisherman. Tony says she will try it, but I doubt she will enjoy it. Nasty things, fish. Before they are cooked, I mean, for of course one must serve a fish course. A cod is nice. Speaking of Cook, Algie, had you not better call for tea? Lady deCourcy must be ravenous after her journey. We shall take tea a little early today."

"You must not rush your tea forward on my account. I am not in the least peckish, ma'am," Cressida said, leaping in while the dowager stopped for breath. "If you will just give me the keys to the little Swiss cottage, I shall go there at once to meet Beau."

"The Swiss cottage!" Lord Dauntry exclaimed in a startled voice.

13

His mama turned an appeasing eye on him. "She means the dower house, Algie. It is the dower house that I am renting to the baroness. Naturally I could not rent out the cottage. It is yours. The dower house is mine. I plan to use the rent money to build a dovecote. Now, what do you think of that? If we give the dammed pigeons a place to roost, they may leave the roof. They are making such a mess of the nice statues.

Lord Dauntry was given no chance to state what he thought of a dovecote. The baroness was on her feet.

"But it was the cottage I particularly wished to rent," she said. "The little wooden place, done up in the Swiss style. I said so in my letters, ma'am. There must be some misunderstanding. I want to be right on the sea. Mr. Montgomery plans to bring his yacht down."

"The dower house *is* on the sea," Lady Dauntry assured her. "It is not five hundred yards west of the cottage. You cannot see it from the water, which is a great blessing since you want peace and quiet, for the people on their yachts always stop and gawk and point at the wooden cottage. It is quite unusual, of course. A sort of folly, really. It would attract even more attention with you there."

Dauntry, whose manners were excellent whatever his mood, rose when the baroness arose. "The cottage is not for hire," he said.

His dark eyes met the baroness's kindling green stare. As Lady Dauntry said to her housekeeper later, "You could have baked an egg in the heat of that look."

"Is the cottage already leased?" Cressida asked curtly.

"It is not leased, nor is it for lease," he replied firmly.

"You use it yourself?" she inquired in a softer tone. If this was the case, she would soon be installed therein. With Dauntry Castle less than half a mile away, Dauntry could be using the cottage only for an occasional outing. He could not be so mean as to keep it from her.

"It is not fit for habitation at the moment. The roof leaks. Squirrels and bats have gotten into the attic."

She knew the cottage roof was done in wooden shingles. It would take but a day to have a few shingles nailed on and the bats and squirrels run off. Cressida had her heart set on living in the cottage. She had never traveled beyond England's shore, and the cottage had a foreign air to it. It would be like holidaying in Switzerland. It had the sweetest little turrets, like a castle in a fairy

15

tale, and a railed balcony coming off the second story, where she had looked forward to setting up a table for afternoon tea while she scanned the sea. Its cove, too, would be ideal for swimming. The duke had told her it was too shallow to take his yacht in, so the gawking banters could not come too close to shore. Beau could anchor his yacht at Beachy Head.

"The dower house is much sounder," Dauntry continued. "And a deal brighter as well. Those leaded windows of the cottage are picturesque, but they are too small for proper illumination. Indeed, all the rooms are small — too small for entertaining. It was built as a retirement home for a widowed aunt in the last century. Her husband had been a sea captain. She wished to be by the sea."

"I do not plan to entertain," Cressida replied reasonably. "I have come to the seashore to escape from society. I do not need much space. The cove there is ideal for swimming."

"The shoreline at the dower house is where we always swam," Dauntry said. "There is also a channel dredged out to allow docking for your cousin's yacht. The cottage does not have mooring facilities."

When reason failed, Cressida changed her

tactics. "But the cottage is so very pretty," she said, adopting a moue that made grown men rush to please her. "I had so looked forward to it. Those turrets reminded me of the books of fairy tales I used to read when I was young, with the heroine locked up in a tower by a wicked guardian."

Dauntry had been observing the baroness for a few years in society. He knew her reputation of wanting her own way, and usually getting it if a gentleman was involved. But her wheedling tricks would not work with him. She had broken his friend Saintbury's heart, leading him on and then jilting him. And Saintbury such an innocent fellow, too. Not an atom of vice in him, but this heartless wench had treated him like dirt under her dainty feet, while society watched and tittered. If she thought to make a jape of Lord Dauntry, she had met her match!

"Like a stage set, it is best seen from a little distance. You can admire it from the dower house," he said politely but firmly.

The baroness surveyed the hand she had been dealt and decided it was time to play her ace. "Well, I thought I was hiring the cottage. If it is not for rent, then I shall just have to go back to Brighton and begin looking again."

As she spoke, she surveyed Dauntry from

17

under her long lashes. She could hardly believe what she saw. He was smiling! He was happy to be rid of her! Half of society had begged her to spend the summer with them, but Lord Dauntry was eager to be rid of her. His mama's invitation had nothing to do with arranging a match, then. She was only to be a replacement for Antonia, who had married and left her mama lonesome.

"I believe Sir George Harcourt has put his place up for rent this summer," Dauntry said at once. "It is not far from here, between Eastbourne and Pevensey."

"Such a pity. I feel a fool," the dowager exclaimed. "It never occurred to me that you meant Algie's little falling-apart place. I made sure it was the dower house you wanted. Why do you not have a look at the dower house while you are here, Lady de-Courcy? It is really quite charming. I have had it all turned out especially for you. And really, you know, it is not very likely you will find another cottage to let at this season."

This gave Cressida the opportunity to retreat from her failed bluff without losing face entirely. "Well, perhaps I shall have a look at it before leaving," she said.

She observed the silent working of Dauntry's lips as he tried to swallow a smile. Hateful man! What was he up to that he was so eager to be rid of her? There was obviously something afoot here that he wished to keep a secret.

"Will you not have some tea before leaving, Lady deCourcy?" he inquired.

"Of course she will," his mama said.

"I am really not at all hungry," Cressida replied with an icy glint in Dauntry direction. "If you will just show me to the dower house, I shall leave now."

"I'll give you directions," Dauntry said. "You will find the door unlocked and the key on the table in the hall. Mama has sent a few servants down, as arranged in your letter."

This went from bad to worse. Dauntry was not even going to accompany her to the dower house.

"I would go with you, but alas, I have a meeting with the parish board in half an hour," he explained, drawing out his watch and glancing at it impatiently.

"I would not dream of inconveniencing you, milord."

They rose, Cressida made her adieu to the dowager, and Dauntry accompanied her to the front door. "I do hope you will still be here when I return, Lady deCourcy."

She turned a sapient eye on him. "Do you indeed, milord? You should be a little careful what you wish for. You may find you get it."

"I certainly hope so, ma'am."

He bowed and handed her over to his model butler. "Tell Lady deCourcy how to get to the dower house, Eaton," he said, and left.

Lady deCourcy was so vexed, she had to ask the butler for directions a second time, for she had not heard a word of his first explanation. Fortunately the route was simple. Just turn left off the main drive and continue down the stone road to the second turning. The first obviously led to the cottage. She took the first turning.

Chapter Two

She soon found herself cut off from the graceful park of the castle, where Repton had designed a winding stream to flow through artful rises and valleys, complete with "side screens" and "distances." Nature had been lent to run riot here, creating a tangled web of wild bushes and nettles with ivy creeping around their feet. She knew the cottage was built into the cliff midway down a rocky incline. Over treetops she could see its shingled roof, which appeared to be in perfect repair. She continued following the road until she reached the cottage, built on a plateau of rock, with a staircase carved into the stone leading to the beach. As there was no sign of life about the place, she alit from her high-perch phaeton to investigate.

Upon close examination she discovered a dozen new delights to entrance her. The whole cottage was made of cedar shingles, weathered to silver by the elements. A frieze of carved woodwork below the roofline displayed tulips and hearts. The same theme was picked up in the painted window shutters. The windows, leaded in the shape of diamonds, twinkled in the sunlight. They were not particularly small windows, either. A refreshing breeze blew off the sea. Another railed balcony coming off the main floor had not been visible from the duke's yacht. On it sat a delicate wrought iron table and chairs in a leafy design, speaking of intimate tea parties. An English garden grew in profusion, with sweet peas and roses clambering over the facade from a bed of ivy, campanulas, gentians, and wild strawberries. Ruby fruit glowed like jewels amid the greenery.

She mounted the steps to the veranda and peered in the window into the main drawing room. Across the room a stone fireplace with a hanging pot leaked just like the sketches in her fairy tales. Brass-fronted firedogs gleamed in the sunlight. There was a cozy-looking stuffed sofa with a table fronting it. On the table sat a wine bottle and two glasses. The cottage was in occasional use, then. Odd the servants had not cleaned up the mess. Where were they? As she pondered this mystery, a shadow fell across the sofa. A man was there! She scampered down from the porch into her highperch phaeton and proceeded to the dower house.

This edifice was all that Lady Dauntry had

claimed, and more. It was nothing less than a mansion done in the same honey-colored brick as the castle, with its own stable and kitchen garden Lady deCourcy was welcomed at the doorway by a stout, bustling housekeeper who introduced herself as Mrs. Armstrong, "But everyone calls me Tory, for Victoria is my name and I have been called Tory forever." The first impression was of red, white, and blue, like the flag. Her hair, pulled into such a tight knob that it gave her eyes an Oriental cast, was white. Her face was as red and round as a radish, and her eyes and gown were blue, the latter mostly covered by a starched white apron.

"I'll just put on the kettle while you have a look around," she said, and bustled off to the kitchen.

Cressida looked about the house, where the servants had been busy with turpentine and beeswax. The woodwork glowed. There was not a mote of dust to be seen anywhere. A quick tour showed her a lofty Blue Saloon with a view of the sea beyond the front windows, a dining room that would seat a dozen, a small library, and large study. She climbed the broad, stately staircase to discover eight handsome bedchambers. Every new elegance made her more determined to remove to the cozy little cottage.

She was tired of elegance; she wanted to rusticate like Marie Antoinette at the Petit Trainon, perhaps buy a cow and play at being a milkmaid. It seemed hard that such a simple request should be denied her when Lady Dauntry had *promised* her the cottage. She returned below when she heard a commotion in the hallway. Miss Wantage and Beau had arrived, the former pale and frowning, propped up by the latter.

Miss Wantage was that unfortunate creature, the poor relation. To add to her woes, she was an aging spinster. She made her home in Bath with Mrs. Barnstable, another cousin, but no one could endure her for twelve months of the year. For six months she was palmed off on anyone who would have her, in three-month leases. Cressida's turn had come. It was either have her for the summer, or be lumbered with her in autumn for the little Season. Knowing that Miss Wantage was an ardent foe of any sort of entertainment, Cressida had opted for the summer.

It was a mystery how Miss Wantage, whose second claim to fame after her religiosity was that she never ate, had grown to such ample proportions. Her face was as wide as a platter. Her blue eyes bore the glow of the religious fanatic, and her lips the accompanying pinched look of disapproval. Her pale brown hair was pulled back in a tight bun and covered with a plain muslin cap. Adornment was abhorrent to the Lord, and certainly to Miss Wantage. Her blue cambric round gown had no ornament save a simple silver cross worn on a black shoe-lace.

"I am rattled to a heap," she said weakly. "I should have gone with you in the phaeton after all, Cressie. At least I would have had fresh air, even if I had been blown to pieces by the wicked sea gales. Just show me to a litter or a truckle bed, and I shell lie down out of your way."

Cressida accompanied her above stairs. "I have put you in the Green Room," Cressida said. "It is the best room and has a lovely view of the sea. I shall have Mrs. Armstrong bring you something to eat."

"I could not eat a bite! You can send her up to me. Perhaps a bit of black tea and some toast, to settle my stomach. My, it is chilly in here!" she exclaimed, shivering. "Odd you did not have a fire laid, but there. You are young and healthy and would not have thought of it. Pay no heed to me."

"I shall ask Mrs. Armstrong to light the fire while she is here."

Miss Wantage felt the bed, found the

feather tick lumpy, and when she had changed into her nightie (after first asking Cressida to just step outside for a moment) detected a wicked draft from the windows. "Perhaps if you would just close those dusty old window hangings, it will cut down on the wind," she suggested, and climbed into bed, drawing the counterpane up to her chin.

Cressida finally escaped to return below to welcome Beau, after first sending Mrs. Armstrong up to Miss Wantage. Beau Montgomery was actually her first cousin, but he had spent summers at Tanglewood after his parents died and was like a young brother to her. Just down from Oxford, he was enjoying a summer of leisure before taking over his estate in Kent, close to Tanglewood.

Despite his long, lean build and interest in matters of toilette, he had no air of the aesthete. His ruddy complexion and bright eyes spoke of a love of the outdoors. The bane of his existence was a crown of golden curls. He wished for black hair, straight for choice, to lend him an air of diablerie. Looked like a dashed girl, with that curl forever tumbling over his forehead.

"This is the last time I undertake a trip with that whiner," he said with great feeling. "We had to stop every mile while she settled her stomach. If it was not hartshorn, it was taking her medicine, which had a decided aroma of ruin, I might add. If you want my opinion, it was the macaroons she never stopped eating that was turning her stomach."

"She is a sad trial to be sure, but never mind."

"I say, Sid, this is something like!" he exclaimed, looking out at the marbled hallway and around the Blue Saloon. "I was afraid the cottage you kept grating of would be a dumpy, moldy little place."

"This is not where we are staying, Beau," she said.

"Let us have tea and you can tell me all about it," he said as Mrs. Armstrong came through the door bearing a loaded silver tray. The tantalizing aroma of fresh gingerbread rose from the tray.

"I have sent Jennet up to deal with your cousin," Tory informed Cressida.

Cressida discovered that the drive had given her an appetite, and enjoyed a good tea, starting with hot buns, clotted cream, and strawberries, and working her way through to the gingerbread.

"How did you find this place?" Cressida asked Beau.

"I went to the castle. Lord Dauntry directed me here."

Cressida put down her teacup with a clatter. "Lord Dauntry? What was *he* doing there?"

"Your wits are gone begging, my girl. He owns the place."

"But he said he had to leave at once for a meeting of the parish council. He could not even wait to accompany me here."

"He must have got back sooner than he expected."

"There has not been time. He never left. He was lying to me. There is something strange going on here, Beau. He said the little cottage I want is falling apart. I stopped there. It is in perfect repair, and with such a sweet little iron table and chairs on the balcony."

"You are better off here, if you want my opinion. A dashed bargain. The place is a toy castle."

"I don't want a castle!" she said petulantly "I want the cottage and I mean to get it."

"Well, if that ain't just like you, Sid, wanting what you can't have. You are becoming spoiled in your old age. All the attention you have been getting in London is going to your head. That is half your trouble. Why, we shall be merry as grigs here. The *Sea Dog* is on her way. Before the week is out we shall be out on the bounding mane. I'll teach you to sail."

This was something to look forward to. Cressida knew she would not find any cottage to suit her better so late in the season. and had decided to remain at the dower house — until she removed to the Swiss cottage.

"Have you decided how many of your servants you'll need?" he asked. "Muffet is fighting it out in the kitchen now with Mrs. Armstrong."

Muffet was Lady deCourcy's butler, and in a pinch, general factotum. It had been decided that he was the only servant who would accompany Cressida to the cottage. Miss Wantage insisted she would act as lady's maid, for she liked to make herself useful. Lady Dauntry had offered the service of a few servants who were familiar with the ways of the cottage, its stove, washing dolly, et cetera.

"Mrs. Armstrong seems capable. I believe I shall leave my housekeeper at Tanglewood to keep an eye on things there. She will need the maids, as there will be a deal of dust and muss with the repairs going forth." And when she removed to the smaller cottage, she would need fewer servants.

"Let us go and settle in, then. I want a ride to look over the place before dinner."

"Ride past the cottage and see if there is anyone about," Cressida said. "I saw a man there earlier. Lord Dauntry said it is not occupied. I should like to know what a bottle of wine and two glasses were doing on the table."

Beau left and Lady deCourcy went above stairs to speak to Miss Wantage. She found her propped up in the bed with a fully loaded tea tray before her. Miss Wantage hastily drew the sandwich she had been devouring under the coverlet and sighed.

"I feel I owe it to you to try to eat a bite to build up my strength," she said. "I wonder if you would just bring that water basin by my bedside, in case I cast up my accounts. I fear I am a notoriously poor traveler. The faintest jarring of the coach upsets my stomach. But I will be better in a day or two, Cressie. Just leave me in peace and quiet. Who is to get out your night things, I'm sure I don't know, for the girl who brought up this tray is as close to an idiot as makes no difference. And you accustomed to so much waiting on. You will have to send to Tanglewood for staff."

"I can manage, Miss Wantage. Just rest. Is there anything else you would like while I am here?"

"Nothing for the moment, dear. Just toast

and tea at bedtime. I shall call this little snack tea and dinner."

"I shall let you get some rest, then."

"Oh, rest! Small chance of that. I can still feel the wheels of your carriage moving under me. Beau *would* encourage John Groom to set a reckless pace. But there, we were all young once."

Cressida escaped to her own room, where she found a mouse of a girl in a mobcap and white apron unpacking her trunks. "Tory told me to do for you until your woman is up and about," she said apologetically.

"Thank you. What is your name, my dear?"

"Jennet."

"Is that your first or last name?"

"Yes, milady."

"I beg your pardon?" Cressida said in confusion.

"Just Jennet, first and last. That's all they call me."

Miss Wantage usually exaggerated to no small degree, but it seemed that in the case of Jennet, she was telling the truth. Jennet was a simpleton. "What is your papa's name?"

"I don't have no pa, nor never had. My ma's name is Mary. She's upstairs maid at the big house."

"Mary Jennet?"

"Yes, milady. And I'm Jennet."

"I see. Well, I shall wear that jonquil gown for dinner this evening, just Jennet."

"That'd be the yeller one, milady?"

"Yes."

There seemed no point quizzing such a witless girl about the cottage, so Cressida went below to speak to Muffet. His usual sluglike complexion had deepened to livid with frustration.

"She has barred me from my own kitchen!" he declared, then, recalling to whom he was speaking, apologized. "Pardon me, missy, but it is more than humankind can bear, to be spoken to in such a way by a *servant*."

Muffet had been deCourcy's butler so long that he considered himself one of the family. He never could remember to call his mistress "milady," but continued to address her as missy, as he had in years gone by.

"You are referring to Mrs. Armstrong, I take it? What, exactly, is the trouble?" Cressida asked.

"I asked to see the silver; she said it had been polished well enough to please Lord Dauntry, and she didn't need checking up on, thank you very much. She was chopping up carrots. I told her you had a particular aversion to carrots. 'She'll like mine,' the hussy said. We must send for Mrs. Hammond at once, for we'll have no peace from that harpy."

"Oh, dear, could you not get along with her, Muffet? It is only for the summer. You know I want Mrs. Hammond to remain at Tanglewood to look after things there."

"Then you must speak to her, missy, and let her know who is in charge here."

"Yes, it might be best to get it settled in the beginning," Cressida said, and rang for Mrs. Armstrong.

Before long, her red face and white hair appeared at the door of the saloon. "You wanted me, milady?" she asked, sparks flashing in her blue eyes.

"Yes, Mrs. Armstrong."

"I'm called Tory, milady. Everyone calls me Tory."

"Tory. We seem to have a little problem here." Cressida had been virtually in charge of running Tanglewood since she was in her teens, and had learned a little something about handling recalcitrant servants. She would try oil first, and if that did not work, then she would issue a decree.

"Muffet has been with me forever. You know how old retainers become set in their ways," she said, smiling and inviting her listener's understanding.

"Croker never had to check up on the silverware at the castle."

"What was your position there, Tory?" she asked pleasantly.

"I was in charge of the entire upstairs — eighty bedrooms, with a dozen girls under me."

"I see, a very responsible position. The next step up would be housekeeper. This summer will be good practice for you. Getting along with the butler is a very important part of housekeeping."

Tory's blue eyes looked sharp at this news. "If it's about them carrots —"

"Muffet is only looking out for my welfare. Between us, we shall keep the peace, eh, Tory?" She gave a conspiratorial smile.

Tory thought a moment, then said, "I'll give him the keys to the wine cellar. Her ladyship — Lady Dauntry — said you must use what is in the cellar here until you make arrangements for yourself."

"Thank you."

"Now, about your groceries, milady, I hope old Muffet won't be trying to tell me where to buy *them*, and me born and bred here on the coast."

"Muffet does not interfere with the meals. You and I shall handle that. We shall meet each morning after breakfast to decide on menus. I quite depend on you to tell me where the best food and bargains are to be had."

"Just ring for me whenever you're ready, milady. And if you've any fault to find with how I run things, I'd appreciate it if you'd tell me yourself, and not old Muffet."

"That is my custom."

Cressida saw that from henceforth Muffet would be known as Old Muffet. She foresaw plentiful rows to come, but for the moment she wanted only a glass of Lady Dauntry's sherry to calm her nerves.

"What time will you be wanting your dinner, then, and how many of you will there be?" Tory asked before leaving.

"Just two of us. Miss Wantage is not feeling well enough to come down. We dine at seven-thirty."

Tory's face puckered in dissatisfaction. "They dine at seven at the castle. I put the roast in —"

"Seven this evening, then, and in future, seven-thirty."

"I'll make a note of it, milady."

Tory bustled out, feeling she had got the better of that round. Cressida sighed and poured herself a glass of sherry, for she did not feel like facing Muffet again so soon.

Chapter Three

The carrots were not served at dinner. Asparagus and peas took their place. Cressida read this as a sign of Tory's eagerness to please and made a mental note to thank her in the morning. With a long evening to be got in, Beau decided to give Cressida her first lesson in sailing. Within an hour her head was reeling with unaccustomed jargon. Beau spoke of "luffing" and "tacking" and "wind on her beam" and something called the "Beaufort scale", which appeared to feature largely in this sport. He drew little sketches of the *Sea Dog*, fully rigged, with arrows denoting the wind coming at it from various directions, and other twisting arrows showing how each sail should be set.

"You want a light trysail, for a heavy one will be impossible to handle during a gale, with your storm jib tossing about," he said, tapping one of the sails on his drawing.

"Perhaps I shall buy a rowboat or have a canoe sent from America," Cressida said.

"You will get the hang of it in no time," Beau assured her. "If I can do it, anyone can.

I hardly ever tip her nowadays. Of course, you must learn to swim before we go out, for there is no counting on a cork jacket to get you to shore if a howler should capsize us in mid-Channel. We might drift about for days," he said merrily.

This ominous speech quite determined Cressida that she would buy a good wide rowboat. But she was interested in learning to swim. She had her costume already made up, and with the privacy the cove provided, she need not fear being watched.

She was about to suggest a game of cards when the door knocker sounded. Although she would not have admitted it for a wilderness of monkeys, the knock was music to her ears. There was such a thing as too much solitude. Her spirits were further improved when she recognized the firm accents of Lord Dauntry in the hallway. Perhaps he had come to give her the cottage!

Her smile could not have been more charming when he was shown in. Cressida observed the exquisite tailoring of his jacket and the broad shoulders beneath it, the intricacy of his immaculate cravat, and noticed how becomingly even a small smile softened the severity of his visage.

Dauntry stopped a moment at the doorway, impressed in spite of himself by the baroness. Cressida, as he thought of her, really was a charmer. Society's spoiled darling looked most alluring with that tousle of crow black curls caressing her cheek and her green eyes glowing with pleasure. Even in the country, she was turned out in the highest kick of fashion, in a jonquil gown that reflected a golden glow on her ivory complexion. He mentally preened himself at her joy in seeing him. He had expected pouts and sulks, and he'd intended to tease the baroness a little.

He made his bows and was shown a seat. "We were just about to have tea," she said, pulling the bell chord to summon Muffet. "Beau has been telling me all about the Beaufort scale."

"Three cheers for Admiral Beaufort," Dauntry replied, apparently familiar with the scale. "I don't knew what we did before Frank analyzed the wind velocity for us. He deserved a medal. Do you sail, ma'am?"

"I am learning," she said. She was not one to make little of her accomplishments.

Beau did that for her. "I am trying to teach her. Ladies don't seem to have the knack for it. Sid threatens to send off to America for a canoe."

"That should be interesting." Dauntry did not care for that "Sid." A man's name ill-suited this paragon of womanhood. She should be a Belle or a Melissa — some sweetly flowing name. He had nothing against Cressida as a name, despite Shakespeare's poor treatment of the character. "False Cressida" he had dubbed her. A giddy girl, a jilt who played with men's hearts for her enjoyment. He might have been describing Lady deCourcy. "Mama sent me down to see how you are going on, Lady deCourcy," he said.

She gave him a saucy smile, revealing a set of pearly white teeth. "Were *you* not curious to see how we are going on, milord? You are a little old to have to be told by your mama what to do."

So she was condescending to flirt with him! This should be interesting. Her anticipatory eyes told him she expected a bantering reply. This being the case, he ignored her taunt. "I had no doubt you were happy with your bargain, once you had seen the dower house," he replied blandly.

"Yes, by Jove," Beau said. "This is something like. Mind you, Sid won't be happy until she gets us turfed out and moved into that little doll's house next door."

Cressida looked expectantly at her guest, who brushed an imaginary speck of dust from his sleeve. Was that why she was flirting and smiling so sweetly? She would catch cold at that. He was no unlicked cub to be led by a lady's smiles. "I trust the servants Mama sent down are working out, Lady de-Courcy?" he asked.

"A few conflicts have arisen, but I straightened them out."

"Tory is a bit of a tyrant. I make no doubt you can handle her," he said with a civil smile, but the glint in his eye revealed his knowledge of Tory's managing disposition.

"I have always found tact goes a long way," she replied demurely. "Except, of course, with the witless." A kindling spark shot from Dauntry's eyes. "I am referring, of course, to Jennet. Has the girl no Christian name?"

"Her name is Janet. Janet Jennet. An unfortunate choice, as she seems unable to distinguish between the two."

"So kind of you to send her to me," she said, still smiling, but he read the sting in her words. She meant he was palming his inferior servants off on her.

"Mama handled those domestic arrangements. We will be happy to have Janet back at the castle if you are unhappy with her. I understand she is an excellent worker despite her mental deficiency. Are there any other

40

complaints you would like to air while you have my ear?"

"Complaints? I was not complaining, milord. It would be too demanding to expect to actually have the use of the house I hired, with the pretty little shutters and the balcony overlooking the sea. I was looking forward to having tea parties on that balcony, but never mind."

"The balcony was a mistake. It receives such a high wind, it would carry you away."

"I should think that alone would be enough to change your mind," she said curtly.

His lips twitched in a amusement. "I do not think only of myself. Society would never forgive me if I caused the loss of its premier Incomparable."

This flattery was accompanied by a bow. Cressida tossed her curls and tuned her attention to the grate. By the time the tea arrived, Dauntry and Beau had fallen into a discussion of luffing and tacking, leaving her to amuse herself. It was not the manner in which she was accustomed to being treated when a gentleman called on her, and an occasional glance from Dauntry suggested that he was aware of his ill manners. "I did not come to pay court to you, miss," that look said.

The tea tray, when it arrived, held only tea. "Ask Tory to send up some of that gingerbread she made this afternoon, Muffet," Cressida said.

Muffet bowed and left. Within five minutes Tory herself appeared at the doorway. She sidled into the room edgeways, like a crab. Her face was an even brighter shade of red than usual.

"I'm sorry about the gingerbread, milady. It's gone."

Cressida just blinked in astonishment. She had no objection to the servants sharing her food, but surely, with so few servants, a large gingerbread could not be gone this soon. "All of it?"

"I threw it out," Tory said. "It didn't rise enough. Sure I wouldn't serve it to the backhouse boy. I'll bake you up a fresh one tomorrow. Meanwhile, there is a bit of plum cake in the larder, if you like."

"That will be fine, thank you."

Tory bustled out, leaving a mystery behind her. What had she done with the gingerbread? It had been good enough to serve that afternoon. Surely a cake did not fall hours after leaving the oven? Cressida was no cook, but she had spent enough hours in her mama's kitchen as a child to know the crucial time for a cake falling was before it was fully baked.

Muffet brought in the plum cake, and the tea party continued. Dauntry had only one cup of tea, made politely banal conversation, then said he must be off.

"Another parish council meeting?" Cressida inquired with a quizzing smile.

He didn't bat an eyelash, although he certainly knew she knew he had lied to her that afternoon. "A social engagement, actually," he replied. "The Forresters are having a rout party this evening. Lady John asked me to invite you. As you had already informed Mama of your wish for solitude, I told her you had come here to rusticate and did not wish to be disturbed."

"How very kind of you," she replied in a thin voice.

"My pleasure," he said with a bow. "I admire, but fear I have not the willpower to emulate your fortitude in seeking a summer's seclusion from society. But then, perhaps I have less need of it." His dark eyes lingered assessingly on her face as he spoke, as though observing the ravages of her many late nights. "One cannot fly with the owls at night and soar with the eagles by day. As my days are strenuous, I do not trot quite so hard as you young — youngish folks at night."

Cressida mentally noted the various slurs on her behavior and age. As if that were not bad enough, he presented them as a pseudo compliment. "No doubt I shall feel the same when I achieve your gray eminence, milord," she said coolly. "Meanwhile, I should be happy to have the choice of accepting or rejecting my own invitations."

"You said explicitly you wished for a quiet summer. Indeed, had Mama suspected you meant to continue the social whirl, throwing the dower house open to receive your many friends and admirers, she would not have rented it."

This was going a good deal too far. "Are you saying I am not even allowed to invite company to my own house?"

"Nothing of the sort. What I am saying is that Mama is too old to be bothered by rowdy parties and your guests tramping through our park and gardens, shooting the rabbits and trampling the flowers."

"What a strange notion you have of my friends, milord. I assure you they are all civilized. You must be thinking of your own guests. I trust your mama will have no objection to Mr. Montgomery sailing his yacht on her ocean?"

His lips quirked in a reluctant smile. "Alas, the ocean is public property. I am sorry if I have offended you by my plain speaking, Baroness. The fact is, Mama is utterly fagged after my sister's wedding, and requires peace and quiet. Naturally Mama — and I — wish to make your visit as enjoyable as possible, so that you do not run off on us."

She strongly suspected his intention was exactly the opposite. He wanted her to be so miserable that she left early, and was using his mama's health as an excuse to curb her pleasure. Lady Dauntry looked hale and hearty. "My visit would be a good deal more enjoyable if I were allowed to live in the cottage I arranged for," she said. "I had a look at the roof on my way here. It seemed in good repair."

"Looks can be deceptive. It leaks. The place is uninhabitable. No one has lived there for years."

"Why don't you have it repaired? It is poor management to allow such a pretty little property to sink into ruin."

To question Lord Danutry's management was as offensive as to question an unmarried lady's age. He had trouble keeping his tongue between his teeth. "I shall bear your advice in mind, madam."

Beau was not sensitive, but he noticed the chill in the atmosphere and wished to warm it. "Is the place haunted?" he asked.

"Only by memories," Dauntry replied without even looking at Beau. His dark eyes were riveted on Cressida.

"You might want to take a look at it on your way home, milord," she said. "Your 'memories' are drinking wine. One of them is such a strong memory, he has assumed a corporeal body. I saw him through the window this afternoon."

Dauntry's face froze in fury. He shot her a look that would freeze fire, then in a silken-soft voice tinged with menace he said, "I would prefer that you not visit the cottage. It is unsafe."

"I am not afraid of ghosts."

"The grounds have not been tended recently. There is a deal of poison ivy and poison oak growing around it. It would be a shame to spoil your visit by falling into poison ivy. And now I must go. Lady John's rout awaits. It promises to be a gay affair. She has had a canopied platform built outdoors. We are to waltz by moonlight. Pity you refuse to come."

Beau began to rise from his seat. "I should like to give that a try, Sid!"

"We were not invited, Beau," she said dampingly.

"And Lady deCourcy is much too soignée

to go where she has not been invited," Dauntry added with a twitch of his lips.

He bowed and left. Cressida waited until she heard the door close before giving vent to her anger. "Beast of a man! How dare he refuse my invitations for me? I should love to waltz by moonlight."

"Pity you told his mama you want to rusticate."

"One can rusticate without becoming a hermit. And furthermore, I should like to know why he is lying to me about the cottage. I saw no poison ivy there. The roof hasn't a loose shingle on it."

"P'raps he has a woman there," Beau said.

"I shouldn't be a bit surprised." She punched a pillow, then looked up, startled. "You have hit the nail on the head, Beau. He has his lightskirt there. Who can she be? I heard nothing of this in London."

"A local woman, very likely."

"Not he! It would be some high flyer. But it was a man I saw inside."

"She would have servants."

"It is very odd about the gingerbread," was her next speech.

"Tory ate it all herself. She is broad as a barn door."

"She could not eat the whole thing. It was very large." She drew a deep sigh. "Pity

47

about the moonlight waltzing party."

Beau stretched his long arms. "What do you say we have an early night? I am a bit fagged after the trip."

"It is only nine o'clock. I shall go and see how Miss Wantage is making out."

"I am for my hammock."

Cressida found Miss Wantage propped up in her bed, still pale and distraught but recovering. "There is something in the attic," she said in a weak voice. "I heard sounds overhead."

Cressida listened but heard nothing. Miss Wantage was the sort of lady who looked under her bed at night before retiring, counted her change twice to make sure the merchants were not cheating her, and invariably heard strange noises when she was alone. Cressida talked to her for a while to calm her, then went to her own room.

She was beginning to think that if she was to be a social pariah here, she must invite a special friend or two to visit her. Not a large party, but a congenial married couple, perhaps, so that they could at least play cards in the evening.

She took up a lamp to examine a few of the guest rooms. The yellow room at the end of the hall proved to be the finest free chamber. Like the rest of the house, it had been cleaned and polished in preparation for her arrival. She drew back the counterpane to check the quality of the sheets. The bed was not made up, but as the house came fully equipped, there would presumably be extra sheets in the linen cupboard.

Finding the evening long, she went below stairs and called for Tory to discuss the linen.

Tory appeared nervous but gave a good account of the situation. "There were only the four good sets of sheets," she said. "There are plenty of old ones in the cupboard. Her ladyship sends them down here when she is through with them at the castle. I put the good ones on your and the master's and Miss Wantage's beds, milady, and asked Jennet to wash the other set."

"Then perhaps tomorrow you will have Jennet make up the yellow room. I may invite a friend to visit."

"Certainly, milady. And about the gingerbread —"

"It was so delicious, perhaps you should bake two the next time."

This was her discreet manner of saying that she had no objection to the servants eating as much as they wished, but she did expect to have sufficient food in the house for herself and any caller. They discussed the matter of acquiring supplies. Tory was eager to handle all the domestic arrangements. She was so relieved to find her mistress reasonable that she said, "I'll ask Old Muffet's advice for anything I'm not sure of, milady. It will save pestering you, and make him feel he's useful."

"What a good idea," Cressida said, swallowing a smile to think what Muffet would make of that piece of condescension.

In the meanwhile, Beau had retired. For lack of anything better to do, she decided to take her new copy of *The Lady's Companion* to bed. She remembered leaving it on the sofa table before dinner, but a look about showed her it was not in the room. She spoke to Muffet, but he had not seen it.

"Jennet was in the saloon," he said suspiciously. "Very likely she's taken it to look at the pictures."

Not wanting to create further discord among the staff, Cressida said she would speak to Jennet in the morning and went to the library to get a novel instead. When she saw the rows of marble-covered gothics from the Minerva Press, she assumed the more worthy tomes were at Dauntry Castle. She selected a book at random and went to bed. The story was a lurid tale of a young lady sent to an isolated house in the country by her wicked guardian to trim her into line. As the heroine lay in her dark bed, listening to the creaking of house timbers and clanking of chains, Cressida began to imagine she heard things, too — in the attic.

Good gracious! She was as bad as Miss Wantage. She blew out the lamp and was soon sound asleep.

Chapter Four

The morning brought new mysteries. Tory, determined to keep on the right side of her mistress, brought the washed and pressed linen for the yellow chamber to show Lady deCourcy while she was still at the breakfast table.

"You might want to have a look at these before I make up the bed in the guest room," she said. "The pillowcases have the family crest worked into them, you see. Done in white, it is hard to see After all that work, I would have done it in a different color to stand out."

"Very nice," Cressida said, lifting a case to examine the fine stitchery. "Did Lady Dauntry do this work herself?"

"Not she! She wouldn't know which end of the needle to put the thread in. She hires Mrs. Campbell, from the village."

As the pillowcase unfolded, Cressida saw a largish brown stain on it. "What is this?" she asked in alarm. At first glance it looked like blood. "We cannot put that on a guest's bed. It looks like —"

Tory's red face deepened to cherry. "It's cocoa!"

"Yes, I believe you're right," Cressida said, taking a closer look.

"That Jennet! She has gone and spilled her cocoa on it whilst she was ironing, and never noticed it, the simpleton. I'll have her wash it again."

"Send her to me, Tory. I am missing a magazine. Muffet thinks she might have taken it. Or perhaps you have seen it?"

Tory's tongue flicked out and touched her lips nervously. "Magazine? No, I didn't see one about. Jennet is not here just now. She's — I sent her to the big house to get eggs. For that gingerbread you wanted."

Even as Tory spoke, Cressida noticed the aroma of gingerbread wafting on the air. The cake was obviously already in the oven.

Tory noticed it, too. "And for an omelette for your lunch," she added. "I put the last of the eggs into the gingerbread this morning, now that I think of it. I must go and have a look at it or it will burn. I'll ask Jennet about *The Lady's Companion.* She will go borrowing things behind a person's back."

On this jumbled excuse, she darted from the room, leaving Cressida in confusion. How did Tory know the name of the magazine if she had not seen it? She was lying, as she was lying about the eggs for the ginger-bread. Was the rest of her story a lie as well, about the cocoa spot on the linen?

Beau soon joined her at the table. "What a night!" he said. "I swear the attic was full of goblins. One of 'em was sobbing its heart out. Did you hear the racket?"

"No. That is — I thought I heard some-thing, but made sure I was imagining it."

"Miss Wantage heard it, too. The place is certainly haunted, whatever Dauntry says. Wantage don't want any breakfast, by the bye. Tory took her up some bread in warm milk. I don't know how she can eat that pap. Daresay she don't. She is feasting off that lunch she had in her basket yesterday. No wonder she is fat as a flawn."

"Then she plans to stay in bed today. She was asleep when I stopped in earlier."

"Such a long trip as fifty miles will take her a week to recover. Pity it wouldn't take the whole summer."

"We should try to be kind to her."

"Aye, for she'll carry tales back to Bath if we ain't. I would like to feel sorry for her, but she sours the milk of human kindness in my breast. It would be easier to be kind to a sinner."

Cressida just shook her head admonish-ingly. "Let us investigate the attic after you have had breakfast, Beau. There is something strange going on here, and I don't think it is a ghost." She told him about the magazine and the mysterious eggs, which were to go into a cake that was already made.

With a mystery to look into, Beau was not tardy in bolting his gammon and eggs. As soon as he was finished, he and Cressida went upstairs, to find the attic door locked.

"Now, that is demmed odd!" he exclaimed. "They must have a family lunatic locked up there."

"Very likely. Beau!" she exclaimed. "You don't think they might have a family lunatic incarcerated at my cottage?"

"It would not surprise me in the least. I know Jennet went trotting over there at first light this morning."

"Really?"

"I saw her leave the house."

"Perhaps she was going only to get the eggs at the castle."

"Then why was she carrying a tray? And besides, she did not go up the gravel road; she cut across the shore. Must have been going to the cottage."

"Good God! Let us get the keys from Muffet and go up to the attic."

Muffet's key chain held many keys, none of which opened the attic door. Cressida went to the saloon and rang for her house-keeper to demand the key.

Tory handed it over with no argument and no discernible sign of reluctance. "I didn't think Old Muffet would want to be climbing all them stairs to the attics. There is nothing but lumber up there," she said.

"I thought I heard a wailing noise last night," Beau said.

"That would be the wind, soughing through the loose windows. It sounds like a banshee some nights."

"But there was no wind last night," Cressida said.

"There is always a wind here on the coast," was Tory's reply. "The house is not haunted, if that is what you are getting at. The cottage is haunted, of course. Folks have seen and heard goings-on there of a dark night."

"Indeed?" Cressida said. And Dauntry had denied the charge flatly!

"Was there anything else I could do for you, milady?"

"That will be all for now, thank you, Tory."

Cressida and Beau darted upstairs, to find an attic much like any ordinary attic. Rooms of discarded lumber, trunks, and racks of old clothing gave off the musty smell of a room long closed up. There was no dust on the floor to reveal footprints. The attic space was divided into two large rooms.

"Obviously no one has been staying here," Cressida said, looking all around and walking into the next room, which was much like the first.

Beau followed her, wedging his way past trunks and broken chairs and summer furniture to the window. "These frames fit like a hand in a glove and are nailed shut for good measure," he said. "I should like to know how they let in any wind. Have a look at this, Sid."

She joined him. He pointed to splatters of candle wax on the floor.

"That might have been there a decade," she said.

Poking about the accumulation of objects near the window, he pulled a pillow and roll of blankets from behind a dresser. When he unrolled the blankets, the missing copy of *The Lady's Companion* fell out at his feet. They exchanged an astonished look.

"I shall speak to Tory about this," Cressida said, and took the magazine down to the saloon to summon her housekeeper once more.

"Are you done with the key, milady?" Tory asked.

"I shall leave it with Muffet. Do you usually keep the door locked, Tory?"

"I do, and I keep the key in my pocket." So saying, she tapped her voluminous apron, producing the rattle of keys.

"Then how did this get up there?" Cressida asked, pointing to the magazine that now rested on the sofa table.

Tory's nervous tongue flicked out. "Up there, was it?" she asked, stalling for time. "It's Jennet," she said, adopting a conspiratorial tone. "She is not quite right in the head. A regular knock-in-the-cradle. She slips away by herself when she is upset. But she's a good worker, mind."

"How did she get the key without your knowing it?"

"It would be when she washed my apron, along with the sheets for the spare bed, wouldn't it? I must have left them in the pocket. I'll speak to her. It won't happen again, milady."

It was clear to the meanest intelligence that Tory was lying. That nervous tongue betrayed her, but as her lively imagination could always find a reply to any question, Cressida released her with a reminder to keep an eye on Jennet.

"Lying in her teeth," Beau said when they were alone. "She knows what is afoot, right enough. She is in it up to her eyes. She was hiding someone up there. Why, it could be a French spy for all we know, here on the coast. You should have asked her about Jennet and the tray."

"She would only fabricate some story."

"What will you do, Sid? Best report her to Lady Dauntry, eh? Or Lord Dauntry. A shame to pester the old girl."

Cressida thought about it for a moment, then said, "No, I shan't report her until I discover the whole. It may be perfectly innocent, a no-good son Tory has given a night's lodging to, or some such thing. I have no wish to get her into trouble. And besides, a mystery will help to pass the time."

"Until my yacht arrives," Beau added. "Meanwhile, why do we not take a drive into the village?"

"Let us go riding instead. I need some exercise."

It had been settled that they were allowed to use the trails on Dauntry's estate. She meant to keep well away from the castle, lest she be accused of trampling the grass, or disturbing Lady Dauntry. Mounted on their bays, they forgot about the mystery while they put the horses through their paces, with the sun warming their shoulders and a breeze cooling their brows.

"Excellent riding! Trust Dauntry," Beau

exclaimed after he landed safely on the far side of a hedge.

After a good run across country, Beau suggested they ride along the coast road to enjoy the ocean view. A sheer cliff fell steeply to the water below. They looked out on a sea of molten copper, glimmering peacefully in the sunlight.

"It is a good thing the dower house has mooring facilities for the *Sea Dog*," Beau said. "I believe the only place hereabouts with easy access to land is that cove on Dauntry's estate. I wonder if it was used for smuggling."

"I doubt Lord Dauntry would permit it. Too toplofty."

"It would explain the man you saw at the cottage, though, and Dauntry's not wanting you to go there."

"You are suggesting that Dauntry is aware of the smuggling, that he condones it?" she asked, surprised at such an allegation. Dauntry was a pillar of the political establishment. Had he been a Tory, he would certainly have been a cabinet minister.

"I daresay he likes his brandy as well as the next fellow."

"No, it cannot be that. That does not account for the other mysteries, the gingerbread disappearing and my magazine being in the attic, and Jennet going to the cottage this morning. Surely it is all tied together somehow. We must keep our eyes and ears open, and see what we can discover, Beau."

"I mean to take a skim over to the cottage the next moonless night all the same, and see if a lugger don't land its cargo. There must be some reason he is so bound and bent to keep you away. Either that, or he has a woman there."

"I shan't wait that long before investigating. I mean to go tonight."

"Then let us take a spin into the village this afternoon to see what sort of a place it is."

Lord Dauntry was waiting for them in the saloon when they returned from their ride. They came in from the stable by the kitchen, thus not meeting Muffet, and found Lord Dauntry sitting at his ease, glancing through Cressida's *Lady's Companion*. Cressida stopped at the doorway and uttered an "Oh" of surprise.

Dauntry rose and bowed. Even in his buckskins and top boots there was no mistaking him for a country gentleman. The cut of Weston's handsome jacket marked him for an out and outer.

"Thinking of becoming a modiste, Lord Dauntry?" Cressida asked.

"Merely an admirer of ladies' fashions," he said, setting the magazine aside. "I hope I did not frighten you, ma'am?" His dark eyes made a quick perusal of his tenant. That burgundy riding habit was becoming to her black hair and fair skin. Unlike the empire gowns, it showed her lithe figure off to full advantage. His eyes skinned appreciatively over her small waist and the feminine flare above and below. Her wind-blown hair was partially covered by a riding hat fashioned in the style of a man's curled beaver. Odd how the masculine hat only enhanced her femininity. Tilted rakishly over one eye, it lent her a hoydenish charm. Her cheeks glowed and her lips were open in surprise.

"Frighten me? You are not so intimidating as all that, milord," she said, coming forward to greet him. They sat down and the visit proper began.

"Did you enjoy your ride?" he asked.

"By Jove, I should say so!" Beau replied. "Excellent riding."

"You should have tried the west meadow. There is a ditch there that might amuse you," Dauntry said.

Cressida noticed that he had been watching them, as he knew they had not been in the west meadow.

"To ride there, we would have had to pass through your park. We were afraid of trampling a daisy. How is your mama this morning?" she asked.

"Much improved, after a quiet night. If I may say so, you are also looking improved after your early night."

"Thank you," she said through thin lips. There, he was doing it again, giving her a compliment spliced with a complaint.

"I have not forgotten your little lecture, Lady deCourcy. You will not want to sink into a hermit after all. I have here an invitation from the vicar's wife, asking you to tea this afternoon. The ladies of the parish usually meet one afternoon a week to discuss church doings while they mend altar cloths and so on. You will decide whether you wish to attend such a raffish affair."

His eyes wore a glow of amusement as he handed her the folded note. The roan was insufferable! Withholding the invitation to a moonlight waltzing party, and urging her to attend this boring tea party.

"Thank you," she said, accepting the note without indicating what her reply would be. For courtesy's sake, she offered Dauntry a glass of wine, thinking he would refuse. He said he would prefer tea, if it was not too much trouble, and settled in comfortably. Cressida asked Muffet to bring tea.

"My nose tells me Tory has baked you the gingerbread she promised," Dauntry said after Muffet left.

"There is something very odd about that gingerbread disappearing," Cressida said, frowning.

Dauntry answered with a chiding look. "We have always found Tory unexceptionable. Our servants are accustomed to certain perquisites. Mama does not mark the level of the wine decanters, or salt the cooking sherry to prevent their drinking it. We must remember servants are people, too. Everyone reacts more favorably to kindness than to criticism."

She lifted a well-arched brow and stared at him. "Now, that philosophy surprises me, coming from you."

He willed down a blush and said haughtily, "If it is your custom to deny the servants a piece of cake —"

"Don't be ridiculous!" she scoffed. "I am not a nipcheese, to begrudge a servant a piece of gingerbread. There are other things going on here that you are — perhaps — unaware of."

He blinked once. "Such as?"

"The magazine in the attic, for starters," Beau said, and told him about their investigation, and the wailing overheard the night before.

"Jennet is a bit odd," he said dismissingly, "but she is a hard worker. As to the sounds, I have never spent a night in an old house that did not squawk and groan."

When Muffet brought the tea tray, Tory followed behind him, bearing a new gingerbread cake eight inches high, the top sprinkled with powdered sugar and decorated with glazed cherries.

"I made this especially for you, milady," she said proudly, and stood by to observe the cake's cutting and serving as if it were a child she wished to see properly launched in the world.

"It is lovely, Tory," Cressida said, and made a fuss over her efforts.

While Cressida served the cake, Tory said to Dauntry, "Her ladyship thought she heard something in the attic last night. She was asking about ghosts. I told her the cottage is haunted by Lavinia."

"Oh, yes," Dauntry said. The two, Tory and Dauntry, exchanged a look that could only be called conspiratorial.

"What sort of ghost is Lavinia?" Cressida asked suspiciously.

Dauntry decided to tease her. "The fact is, I had a friend — a lady friend — staying there some time ago."

"And did she die of boredom, or was it the gale on the balcony that did her in?"

Dauntry's lips moved unsteadily. "The gale," he replied. "You must know it is usually those who die a violent death who return to haunt. I promise you, Lavinia was never bored."

"I remember the gale well," Tory said. "That awful gale in the last century."

"The last century! You were a precocious lad!" Cressida said, blinking in surprise.

Dauntry swallowed his ire and said to Tory, "Your gingerbread looks delicious."

"It is your cook's receipt. I know how to do more than make a bed and dust a room," she informed his lordship. "I could run a whole house with no trouble at all."

"Don't let us keep you from your multifarious duties below stairs," he said, smiling graciously.

"I'd best get a hand on Jennet, or there is no saying what the moonling will be at." So saying, she bustled importantly from the room.

Quell now," Dauntry said, "the cat is out of the bag. The cottage is nothing else but a love nest. Papa had it done up in a style to suit his *chère amie.* It is totally unsuitable to a lady. As you are not a deb, Lady deCourcy, I can admit that it is still used from time to time."

His impassive face revealed not a shred of shame at this admission. It was Cressida who blushed.

Beau cleared his throat and said, "A great day for sailing. I wish my *Sea Dog* were here."

"When do you expect it?" Dauntry asked, happy to quit the former subject.

"My captain was having the mainmast tightened. It worked itself loose of its moorings."

The talk turned to sailing, after which Dauntry escaped.

"Liar," Cressida said as soon as he had quit the door. "If someone had been blown off that balcony, they would have had it removed, or closed in at least."

"It is as I've said all along; Dauntry has a lightskirt there."

"Perhaps," she said pensively.

It was by no means impossible — but it did not account for the other little mysteries that floated about the house.

"I shall decline this invitation from the vicar's wife, as we have planned to go to the village this afternoon. Their scandal broth will all be of ladies who are unknown to me. I must be sure to call on her another time, as she has invited me, however."

Beau went out to observe the wind and Cressida wrote to the vicar's wife. At Dauntry Castle, Lord Dauntry sat mentally running over the local belles, wondering if he should import one of them into the *chalet* for the summer, to lend credence to the tale he had told Cressida. All things considered, he thought a female on the premises might be more bother than good. With the smugglers about from time to time, the situation might become even more complicated. Lady deCourcy was proving trouble enough. But he was by no means eager to see her leave the dower house.

He was pleased that the rumors he had set afoot about a ghost at the cottage had thrived. That kept the locals away, but he feared it would only prove an incentive to Lady deCourcy. He smiled to remember that Tory had devised an actual identity for the ghost. She had been wearing a very knowing look. Tory must have seen a lugger stop at the dock and assumed he was smuggling brandy. She would sell her soul to Satan to protect any of the family, but he was sorry she had put the date of the gale so far in the past. Lady deCourcy would think him an antique. Not that she had believed a word of it. The image of Lady deCourcy lingered in his mind long after he had forgotten the rest of the visit.

Chapter Five

Miss Wantage loved to visit the shops nearly as much as she loved complaining. Her hostess could usually be shamed into buying her some trifle. She was sorely tempted to recover her health when she learned of the projected trip to Beachy Head, but in the end sloth won out and she got no farther than to a chair by the window, where one look at the cold sea sent her back to her nice warm bed. Cressida's generosity regarding material for a new fall suit could be appealed to another time.

Cressida and Beau were about to leave, when a rattle of the door knocker delayed them.

"I am surprised Lord Dauntry has not posted a Keep Off sign at the gate to protect us from callers," Cressida snipped.

Before Beau could reply, a young gentleman's voice was heard in the hallway.

"No need to show me in, my good man. I am no stranger here," the brash voice said.

Muffet followed behind, wearing a face of deep disapproval. "Mr. Brewster to see your ladyship," he announced.

Cressida looked at a young whelp rigged out in what perhaps passed for the highest kick of fashion in the provinces. His jacket was not by Weston. Mr. Weston would never have violated an ell of blue Bath cloth by wadding the shoulders out of all proportion as her caller's tailor had done, nor would he have allowed brass buttons of such an enormous size. The caller's tawny hair was artfully brushed over his forehead in the Brutus do. A pair of blue eyes darted about the room as if he expected someone to pop out at him.

"I am Allan Brewster," he said with a jerky bow. "You must be Lady deCourcy. I have been waiting forever to meet you."

"How do you do. This is my cousin, Mr. Montgomery," she said, wondering if she should have Muffet eject the man. Muffet stood in the doorway, awaiting missy's decision. She listened to hear what her caller had to say before giving Muffet the nod.

"I am Lady Dauntry's godson," Brewster said, which got him the offer of a chair. Cressida gave an infinitesimal nod of her head, and Muffet retired. "I live at the abbey just three miles down the road," he added. She waited for an invitation to call on his mama, but she waited in vain. "So, how do you like

71

the place so far, Lady deCourcy?"

"I just arrived yesterday. My cousin and I were about to go to the village," she said, hoping he could take such a broad hint.

"It is not worth the trip," he informed her. "Nothing but the hotel, a coastguard station, Mullins's Drapery Shop, and a run-down old church. And, of course, a few pokey little shops. Nothing to tempt an out and outer. Where you want to go for shopping is Brighton. It is only a minute away."

"I have just escaped from Brighton," she replied. "I did not come here to shop, but for peace and quiet. Away from callers, you know," she added, hoping to get rid of him without resorting to outright rudeness.

"By Jove, you have come to the right place for that. There is never a thing going on here. Dull as ditch water. I say, would you mind terribly if I — er — washed my hands?"

"Certainly. I shall call the butler."

Brewster was already on his feet. "Not necessary, milady. I have been running tame here since I was in short coats. My old aunt Annie battened herself on Lady Dauntry until she cocked up her toes a few years ago."

So saying, he fled out the door. "That is one caller I would not have minded Lord Dauntry's turning off," she said to Beau.

"The fellow might be anyone, cheeky

devil. I mean to see what he is up to," Beau said, and went out after him.

Mr. Brewster was just talking to Jennet, however. The girl obviously knew him, for she was smiling and chatting. "No, I never seen hide nor hair of her," she was saying, apparently discussing some mutual acquaintance.

Beau returned to the saloon. "The servants seem to know him, all right. I wonder if he sails. I shall ask him when he returns."

"He seems a ramshackle fellow," Cressida said. But then, many of Beau's friends seemed ramshackle to her. Perhaps she *was* getting old. Dauntry's little jibe still rankled. Young*ish*, he had called her.

"I wish he would come back — and leave," Beau said after a few moments. He paced the saloon twice, stared out the window, then glanced at his watch. "It seems he stopped only to use the necessary. What the deuce is keeping him?"

After ten minutes and several tours of the saloon, it began to seem that Mr. Brewster was indeed up to no good. Cressida went into the hallway to discover him hovering at the top of the stairway to the kitchen with his ears cocked. What was he listening for? At the same moment, Tory was just coming down the front stairs. She looked at Mr.

Brewster as if he were a tiger.

"Tory!" he exclaimed. "What the devil are you doing here? Have you been banished from the castle?" Without waiting for a reply, he rushed on. "You will be surprised to see old Allan Brewster here, but here I am. Just dropped in to pay my respects to Lady deCourcy. Well, I must be off. If you happen to run into Lord Harold, give him my respects. And his good wife as well. Be sure to tell Tony I was asking for her. I would not want her to take a pet. Fancy Harold being shackled. I will be next, I daresay. If I don't watch what I am about, some lady will nab me. Well, I am off."

He darted to the hall table, retrieved his curled beaver, gave Cressida another jerky bow, and fled out the door as if the law were at his heels.

"What a strange young man," Cressida said. "And what was he doing at the stairs to the kitchen? Do you know this Allan Brewster, Tory?"

"Allan Brewster?" she said with a shocked face. "Why, I have known him from the egg, milady. A very good fellow."

"It is odd he did not know of Tony's wedding trip if he is such a friend of the family."

"No doubt he thought she had got cold feet and cut the trip short. Lady Antonia is a great stay-at-home, you must know. Mr. Brewster is quite a favorite of the Dauntry's. I fancy her ladyship asked him to drop in to pay his respects. I shall just count the spoons." On this unsettling speech, she bustled off.

Lady Dauntry *asked* him to call when she was so concerned for her tenant's privacy? It did not seem at all likely to Cressida.

Beau came into the hallway. "Has he gone?" he asked.

"Yes, he just ran off. Shall we go?"

Muffet had already called the carriage. As it was a short trip, they had elected to take Cressida's phaeton. They discussed the visit during the short drive. Beachy Head, a chalk headland rising precipitously from the sea, had an impressive air of grandeur. The surrounding village, however, was much as Mr. Brewster had described it.

They looked at the old Norman church and went into Mullins's Drapery Shop, the busiest spot in town. Cressida found some pretty silk threads and decided to take them home to Miss Wantage, who was a keen needlewoman. While she made her purchase, Beau fell into idle conversation with a young gentleman in the line of customers behind her and introduced himself.

"Ah, you are staying at the Dauntrys'

dower house!" the gentleman exclaimed. "I have been wishing to call, but Lady Dauntry mentioned Lady deCourcy wished for seclusion."

"Not that much seclusion. Dash it, we are bored to flinders. You must come out for tea one day soon," Beau said.

Cressida had examined the gentleman and found him to be unexceptionable. He was well if modestly dressed, well spoken, and wore an air of gentility. Of equal importance, Beau was obviously missing his friends.

"I shall introduce you to her now," Beau said as Cressida turned to them. "Sid, this is — oh, I don't believe I caught your name, sir."

"Allan Brewster," the gentleman said with a very civil bow.

He wondered why his new acquaintances were staring at him as if he had sprouted horns. The busy clerk said, "Ahem — can I help you, Mr. Brewster?"

"Pardon me a moment, ma'am," he said, and executed his purchase.

When he rejoined them, he said uncertainly, "Is something wrong, Lady deCourcy?"

"But — are there two Allan Brewsters in the neighborhood?" she asked.

"No, my papa is George Brewster. I have

76

an uncle Derwent and three sisters, but I am the only Allan Brewster."

"Then there is someone impersonating you," Beau said, "and he called on us not an hour ago. Talk about brass! You ought to have him arrested."

"He seemed to know the house and servants," Cressida added in perplexity.

"What did he look like?" Mr. Brewster asked.

"He was about your age and general size, a little taller than average, with light brown hair and blue eyes," Cressida said.

"That sounds like me," Brewster said, frowning. Then a reluctant smile tugged at his lips. "James Melbury!" he exclaimed. "He is a regular jokesmith. I heard he was off to Bath, but if he caught wind of your visit, milady, he would do anything to meet you. He is fond of the ladies, to tell the truth. But I fancy you know that by now."

"I did not take him for a flirt," she said, mentally reviewing his brief visit. "He seemed a brash sort of fellow."

"He would ask old Queen Charlotte herself to stand up and jig it and think nothing of it. He knew he would not be allowed through the doorjamb if he used his own name, so he has used mine, the dastard. I shall ring a peal over Melbury when I catch him. I hope you counted the spoons when he left. He is a famous thief."

As Tory had implied this same fondness for cutlery in her caller, Cressida assumed the mysterious man was indeed Mr. Melbury.

"Why is he not in jail, if he is a thief?" she asked.

"You must not take me too literally, ma'am. I only meant I would not lend him any money if I were you, or sell him anything on tick. I am still waiting for my two hundred guineas for a horse I sold him a year ago, but I doubt he actually steals from stores or strangers, only from his friends."

"I shall see that he don't become a friend of mine," Beau said.

"Oh, there will be no avoiding him. He is invited everywhere," Brewster said, shaking his head ruefully. "He is Lady Dauntry's godson, you see, and Dauntry's cousin, so they always settle up his accounts at the shops eventually. That keeps him out of the roundhouse, and spares the rest of us a rise in the parish rates. They did not repay me for the mount, though. Dauntry said I ought to have known better, and so I ought."

"You should demand the horse back," Beau said.

"It was sold and out of the parish before

nightfall," Brewster replied.

"It is odd he would use your name when we shall be meeting him again," Cressida said, frowning.

"It is not likely you will see him again, ma'am. He was about to leave for Bath last time I spoke to him. I made sure he would be gone by now. He saved one last prank to pull off before leaving. He wanted to meet you first. One can hardly blame him for that," he added with a shy smile.

"Good riddance, say I," Beau declared, and began discussing a future meeting with Mr. Brewster.

As she approved of this Mr. Brewster, Cressida invited him to call; Mr. Brewster returned that his mama would be delighted if Lady deCourcy would care to drop in the next time she was in Beachy Head, and they parted on the best of terms.

"I shall roast Dauntry about this the next time we meet," Cressida said, laughing about the incident.

"All families have their dirty dishes," Beau reminded her. "I would not want the Dauntrys to meet Gerald Charmsworth."

This derelict cousin had ran off with an actress and was happily living in sin in London, where he and polite society ignored each other.

As the day was fine and the hour early, they elected to walk three-quarters of a mile east to Birling Gap, with the cliffs called the Seven Sisters beyond. The wild scenery and the stretching sea were still a novelty to them.

"One of Devonshire's seats in nearby," Cressida mentioned. "Comptom Place, but I don't believe he is in residence. He mentioned going to Chatsworth."

By the time they had executed the walk back to Beachy Head over rough terrain, they were ready to go home.

Cressida allowed her cousin to take the reins for the return trip, which left her free to think and talk. "You know, Beau," she said, "Tory knew who our caller was. Why did she let us believe he was Mr. Brewster? Why did she connive with him to fool us?"

"Because he is Dauntry's cousin, I expect. They seem to dote on the fellow."

"I must have a word with her when we return. I will not be lied to by my own servants."

"She lied about the ghost, two, and the gingerbread cake. As I think it over, she has lied a blue streak ever since we got here."

"I mean serious things. Melbury might have stolen something from the house, and we will be accused of it."

As soon as she had removed her bonnet, Cressida asked Muffet to send Tory to her in the saloon. Tory's ruby face wore an air of guilt. "What could I do for you, milady?" she asked in a strained voice.

"Were any spoons missing after our caller's visit, Tory?"

"Oh, no, ma'am. I did a whole inventory. He didn't pocket a thing, not so much as a salt cellar."

"You are aware that our caller was not Allan Brewster, but James Melbury, I think?"

"I thought he was looking very like Melbury," was her foolish reply.

"You knew it was Melbury!" Cressida said crossly.

Tory looked in guilty confusion. "He said he was Allan Brewster. You heard him yourself. I'm sure it is not for me to question my betters. Lord Dauntry's cousin, after all."

"It is for you to protect your mistress, Tory. You knew that neither Muffet nor I would recognize the man. It was very wrong of you to connive with Melbury in pulling off this impersonation."

"It was only a joke, milady. We all like a little joke from time to time. Melbury is a famous jokesmith," she said with a harried frown that spoke of her enjoyment of this prank.

"This is carrying a joke too far," Beau said sternly.

"Sure and I counted every inch of the silverware as soon as ever he left. And about them noises in the attic," she added, hoping to alleviate her culpability in the affair of the impersonation, "it was bats. Very likely Jennet's cat slipped up the stairs while the door was ajar and got to chasing them about."

"You got the key from Muffet?" Cressida asked.

The crimson face turned a shade deeper. "There happened to be a spare key. I wanted to go up and have a look for myself, for it bothered me to hear your sleep was disturbed by the bats knocking about."

"I did not see any bats," Cressida said.

"That would be because Jennet's cat got them all."

There was obviously no point in discussing it further with this accomplished liar. She had not suddenly found a spare key to the attic. She had had one all along. As Muffet also had a key now, however, she would not press the point, but only keep a sharp eye on the attic in the future.

"Let me bring you a nice cup of tea and

some of my gingerbread," Tory said.

Cressida accepted this peace offering, but she knew she had not gotten to the bottom of the strange goings-on at the dower house.

Chapter Six

Another dull evening stretched before Cressida and her cousin, alleviated — or, more accurately, aggravated — by the presence of Miss Wantage, who had hobbled to the table for dinner, wrapped in her white woolen shawl, to indicate her status of recuperating invalid. When she was quite well, the shawl would be exchanged for a blue one. Miss Wantage was, of course, interested in their caller, but once she learned he was Lady Dauntry's godson, she refused to find much ill in him. She was a keen admirer of a title.

"Youth and high spirits go together. 'To flaming youth let virtue be as wax,' as dear Shakespeare said." Miss Wantage was not really so abandoned in her morals as this would suggest. She had once had a sentimental verse published in *The Lady's Companion*, since which time she was much given to quotations, regardless of their suitability.

"That ain't what you said when I got sent down from Oxford," Beau reminded her.

"Nor when Cressida took to wearing moistened gowns that clung so vulgarly," Miss

Wantage agreed, "but playful high spirits of this sort are harmless."

She then began lamenting having missed the visit to Beachy Head in so pointed a manner, Cressida offered to take her the next day.

"For those silks you brought me, dear — and pray do not take this as a complaint, for I am sure the thought was very kind — but the colors are just a little vulgar. They hurt these poor old eyes. You know I always prefer the less violent pastel shades for my work. That glaring bile yellow and royal blue look so very common in a piece of embroidery. One does not find them in nature," she said quite inaccurately.

But there was no arguing with Miss Wantage when it came to embroidery. If the shade "hurt her poor old eyes," it was vulgar, and that was that.

"Ah, turbot in white sauce again," was her joyless comment when the fish was served "How often one is confronted with it in Bath. I had thought we might at least have some different seafood here by the sea, but I am sure Mrs. Armstrong has made the sauce very nicely. Hardly lumpy at all," she said, poking her fork about with obvious distaste. She took two bites and set her fork down.

"Very likely it is the ferocious wind off the

sea that makes the mutton so tough," was her forgiving comment on the meat.

"An apple tart! How — rustic," she said weakly when the dessert was served. "I do think it a mistake to serve apples in June. Best wait until July or August, when the first new crop appears. A nice blancmange or syllabub would have suited me better at this time. All that grease in the crust sits heavily on a queasy stomach."

Before long, the three were installed in the Blue Saloon, where Miss Wantage required a fire to take the "damp chill" off the air. With her woolen shawl tucked around her, she drew out her embroidery, tsked at the vulgar yellows and blues, and asked Beau to thread a needle for her with the last piece of her pale pink thread, for her poor eyes, which could spot lechery a mile away, were worse than useless when it came to threading a needle.

"Now, isn't this cozy!" she said, smiling at her cousins. "So much better than all the mad dashing about of London. We will get your sallow complexion brightened up in no time, Cressida."

The only sound in the room for the next minute was the ticking of the longcase clock in the corner and the snapping of logs in the grate.

"One is hardly aware of the wretched pounding of the sea tonight," Miss Wantage said, poking her needle into her linen. "I was afraid, last night, that I would never sleep a wink until we got away, but tonight it is not bad at all. I have had Jennet move me from that drafty room facing the sea, Cressida. I am sure it is no odds to you where I lay my poor old head. The yellow room will do nicely, and perhaps the racket from the attic will be somewhat subdued in another room."

"Whatever you like, Miss Wantage," Cressida said, although she had told Miss Wantage that very morning that she planned to use the yellow room for company. Perhaps she had forgotten. One must be charitable.

After another moment Miss Wantage cast a reproving look on her youthful companions. "The devil makes work for idle hands, children. Why do you not try a piece of embroidery, Cressida? Time to begin accumulating your hope chest. You never know, you might nab someone yet, as you still have not put on your caps at five and twenty. I donned mine at twenty-one. By that age a lady knows. And you, Beau, can you not stop fidgeting? It is so common. You have not so much as opened the journal you brought from Beachy Head. A gentleman ought to keep himself au courant with what is afoot in the world."

Beau's lips clenched. He rose and said, "Excuse me, ladies. I have to write a few letters." Then he fled the room.

Cressida had no sooner picked up the journal and began to glance through it than Miss Wantage set aside her embroidery. "Oh, *you* are reading the journal," she said in a thin voice. "I had wanted to glance at the court news, but pray do not let me interrupt you."

Cressida counted to ten and handed over the journal. "I shall get a book from the library," she said, to escape.

"You will find nothing worth reading there, Cressida. I took a peek in this afternoon while you were out. If you want something to read, I have Hannah More's latest book of essays here in my sewing basket. Very uplifting, to see someone taking a thought to the evils of mankind. Perhaps you will read it to me while I stitch. Reading maketh a full man."

"I thought you wanted to read the court news."

" 'Vanity of vanities; all is vanity.' Ecclesiastes, I believe. One feels the attraction of court. I own it is a weakness, but we are only frail human flesh after all. We might profit from the essay on idleness," she said with a pointed look.

Cressida read two pages, after which time Miss Wantage smiled a painful smile. "It is well you have independent means, my dear, for you would never do as a ladies' companion. You really ought to try to cultivate your voice a little. I believe I shall turn in now. I cannot think what has given me back my headache."

So saying, she picked up the journal and left Hannah More's essays behind. While Cressida was still drawing a sigh of relief, Beau's head peered around the corner.

"Is she gone for the night?" he asked.

"Yes, to bed, thank goodness."

"What a take-in, Cousin Alice telling me Miss Wantage was down as a nail. She is nothing else but a Jeremiah in skirts. Alice said it only to be rid of her."

"And who can blame Alice?" Cressida said with feeling. "I warned you what she was like. This was a wretched idea, coming here, Beau. It makes me appreciate Brighton."

"And London, or even Tanglewood. Tomorrow we shall call on the Brewsters, if they don't come here first."

"I mean to call on Lady Dauntry and speak to her about Melbury as well, in case anything is missing from the house."

As she spoke, the door knocker sounded. Cressida's expression of ennui faded, to be replaced with an ill-concealed smile of anticipation. Dauntry!

E'er long, he was shown in. "What a delightfully domestic scene," he said as his eyes alit on Hannah More's latest tract. "The diversity of your interests astonishes me, Lady deCourcy. I had not taken you for a reformer."

"It belongs to Miss Wantage," Beau said. "You have not had the pleasure of meeting Cressida's chaperon."

"Pleasure!" Cressida said in astonishment. "The woman is a public nuisance. She does nothing but scold and carp on nothings."

Dauntry's nostrils pinched in disapproval. "That is poor reward for the lady, after she has been kind enough to leave her home and chaperon you for the summer, Lady deCourcy. It would be more proper for you to behave in a manner that does not cause her to scold."

"I am not quite ready to join the Clapham sect," she replied in Arctic accents. "Won't you take a seat, milord, or did you come only to take up where Miss Wantage left off?"

"I would not dare to presume so far on your patience." He sat down, turning to face Cressida. "That sparkle in your eyes tells me it is my turn to receive a scold. And the servants' grapevine tells me why. I understand you have suffered a call from Melbury."

She was sorry he had taken the wind out of her sails. "Indeed we have, and impersonating Mr. Brewster, if you please."

"He is a wretched fellow. If he comes again, send him up to the castle. I had thought we were rid of Melbury for the summer. I bribed Cousin Beatty to invite him to Bath just after Tony's wedding. How did you catch on to Melbury so quickly? But my wits are gone begging. Tory, of course, would have told you."

"Oh, no. Your servant went along with the game — despite your high opinion of her," Cressida informed him.

"We met Allan Brewster in town," Beau said, and gave some details of the encounter. "I say, Lord Dauntry, would you like a glass of wine? Or a cup of tea? The tea tray ought to be arriving any minute."

"I dropped in only to explain — and apologize — for Cousin Melbury." He pulled at his collar, glancing at the raging fire in the grate.

"Oh, don't go!" Beau exclaimed. "We are as dead as doorknobs here. Don't mind the fire. We can remove to the other side of the

91

room. It is Miss Wantage, you see. She is always freezing. She will be cold in Hades — not that she will go to Hades, but if she makes it through the pearly gates, it will be no heaven for me."

Cressida noticed that Dauntry did not chide Beau for speaking ill of their chaperon. Why did he feel free to criticize her, and not Beau? Dauntry looked a question to Cressida. "Do stay," she said with an air of indifference. Then added, "Unless you are en route to some other social do, of course."

He rose and offered her his hand to remove to the far side of the room. The tea tray arrived, and Cressida occupied herself with the pouring, while Dauntry admired the ladylike movements of her delicate wrists and fingers.

"No moonlight waltzing party this evening," he said. "But if you have so soon discovered the limits of your own resources, why did you not attend the party at the vicarage?"

"Because I did not feel like it," she replied with a glare that dared him to object.

"If you have had enough of your own company and are ready to meet the local society, Mama has planned a small dinner and rout party for next week. We would be honored if you would attend."

"I should say so!" Beau exclaimed. "We are finding our own company pretty dull, I can tell you."

"We were not meant to live alone, cut off from society," Dauntry said forgivingly. Especially such charmers as Lady deCourcy. She was looking particularly well now that she had put off her sulks.

"What I ought to have done was set up a course of study and brought some books with me," she said, "for I know I am as ignorant as a swan when it comes to weighty matters like polities. I went to the House once and could not make heads or tails of it."

"Nor can I, half the time," Dauntry admitted. "As to your course of reading, I fear you will find nothing of an improving nature here. Cousin Annie was the last occupant. Gothic novels were her main vehicle of culture. I have a fair to middling library at the castle. You must feel free to visit it. I am not as familiar with the library as I ought to be. I spend most of my time in London."

"Are you here for the whole summer?" Cressida asked, and listened with interest for his reply.

"I shall be back and forth as necessary. I hope to spend the weekends here at least." He noticed her smile at his answer. Despite her expressed wish for privacy, Lady de-

Courcy was not immune to dalliance.

"We shall have a picnic one Saturday," she said.

"But not this Saturday, I hope, or I shall miss it. I must go to London tomorrow."

"Next weekend, then, weather permitting."

"My yacht will be here by then," Beau said. "Don't count on me, unless you want to have your picnic aboard ship."

"You know Miss Wantage would not step foot aboard the *Sea Dog*, Beau," she chided.

"Precisely! We don't want her Friday face complaining of gales and drowning, to say nothing of sand and ants. What good is a picnic without sand and ants?"

"Did you plan to supply sand and ants aboard your yacht?" she asked.

"Wind and waves will do as well. So long as it ain't just sitting at a dull table."

"One other reason I called," Dauntry said, turning to Beau. "I wanted to warn you to keep your yacht away from the cottage. There are rocks close to the surface there. They are not visible in the dark water. I have the place marked out with buoys, but really you are better to keep away from it entirely."

"I thank you for the warning, sir."

Dauntry noticed Cressida's interest when he mentioned the cottage. He had hoped that subject was at an end, but within two seconds she had begun pestering him again.

"If you plan to spend most of the week in London, will the cottage be empty?" she asked. "Come now, Dauntry, don't stare!" she added with a quizzing smile. "It was you who intimated you had a friend installed there. As you so kindly pointed out, I am not a deb. Surely you would have more opportunity to visit your friend five days a week in London than only two on the weekends."

"I am kept pretty busy in London."

"The House will be in recess come July, if it is not already."

"Most of the members will return to their constituency, but the inner circle still meets to plot strategies and counterstrategies. No rest for the wicked — and no cottage for the baroness, I fear. So you met young Brewster," he said, quickly changing the subject. "He is the leading bachelor of the parish. I expect he will soon be enlivening your dull evenings. You want to have him show you over his abbey. A very fine building. The east wing . . ."

He spoke on of Brewster's estate while Cressida half listened, but her mind was on Dauntry's intransigence. She did not believe he had a *chère amie* at the cottage. He would have had his gardener tidy up the grounds if the place was occupied. The woman would be seen about the place. Beau spent a good deal of time on the coast, looking out for the *Sea Dog*'s arrival, and he had reported no sign of life at the cottage.

Dauntry remained for half an hour, at which time he said he had to leave for London early in the morning and must be off. "No need to send for my mount. I walked down," he said. He thanked them for the tea, said he looked forward to returning soon, and left.

"This room is still too warm," Cressida said, trying to poke the fire out. "Let us go out for a breath of air before retiring."

They walked down to the shore, breathing in the fresh, moist air. A new moon cast a sparkling white net on the calm water. About half a mile from shore, a small boat lay nearly becalmed in the still air. Waves washed quietly on the pebble beach. Some other sound was there as well, a sound not loud but regular.

"What is that?" Beau asked. "It sounds like footsteps. Someone is coming."

A delicious shiver scampered up Cressida's spine as she and Beau took cover under a spreading willow. They waited, peering through the drooping branches into the shadows, but no one appeared. In fact, the

96

footsteps were receding. Beau darted out to see if he could spot the intruder. He was back in an instant.

"It is Dauntry!" he exclaimed in a low whisper. "He ain't returning to the castle at all. He is going to the cottage. There is no place else he could be going along this stretch of beach."

"So he does have a woman there," Cressida said, and was aware of an angry heart inside her.

"Devil a bit of it. It is something else. Let us follow along and see whom he meets."

"It is of no interest to me," she said, and strode back into the house.

Chapter Seven

It took Beau two minutes to convince Cressida to accompany him to the chalet, and another five for her to run upstairs and change her pale rose evening gown for a muslin day dress more suitable to rough usage.

"Dash it, he will be gone by the time we get there," Beau complained when she reappeared. "If that ain't just like a lady, having to change her gown at the last minute."

"I will not destroy my new rose gown for Lord Dauntry. He is not worth it," she said haughtily, and stalked into the hallway.

"The moonlight is so lovely, we are going out for a walk along the shore, Muffet," she said in a calmer voice to her butler as they hurried out.

Muffet was not so easily misled. Missy would not be running like a filly to look at the moonlight. He had a fair notion where she was going, and followed after her, taking up a walking stick from the Chinese urn by the door in case there should be blows involved in the lunar excursion. The only error

98

in Muffet's reading of the outing was that he lay the blame on Melbury, not his cousin, Dauntry. Muffet assumed they had some knowledge that Melbury meant to return and were endeavoring to catch him red-handed.

Cressida had not thought to change her shoes and found the walking rough over the shingle beach in her kid evening slippers. They saw from a distance of a hundred feet that no lights were lit at the cottage. The only illumination was the ghostly reflection from the dark panes of glass. They stopped to look up and down the beach.

"We've lost him," Beau said in disgust. "Next time I shall go by myself. I wager that was a smuggling vessel we saw tacking toward Beachy Head."

"If it was, they did not unload any brandy," she pointed out. Neither the shore nor the steps of the cottage held any contraband.

"Perhaps Dauntry was placing his order for next time, or just bought a barrel from them. It might be around here someplace. Let us have a look."

They climbed the stone staircase cut into the cliff, up to the plateau where the cottage stood. They poked around the shrubbery without finding anything.

"He might have taken it inside," was Beau's next idea.

Cressida had begun to lose interest. If Dauntry was doing nothing worse than buying a barrel of brandy, it was of no interest to her. She was relieved to see there was no female staying at the cottage, but she had to wonder why he had intimated there was. If he cared for her good opinion, he would have been at pains to hide it. Of course, Dauntry had no interest in her good opinion. He had made that crystal clear.

While she reviewed these thoughts, Beau tiptoed up the four stairs to the front door and opened it.

"It ain't even locked!" he called to Cressida. "Let us just go in and see if we can find the brandy."

"That is none of our concern," she said impatiently.

"Is it not, by Jove? He can scarcely refuse getting me a barrel when he has one hidden away himself."

"You don't drink brandy, Beau."

"No, but I should like to have a hogshead aboard to offer the fellows a drink when they come. All the crack."

Even as he spoke, he was opening the door and slipping inside. Cressida followed a few paces behind. In the hallway, she stopped to peer around. The blinds were not drawn. Moonlight cast a wan light on the small parlor. She could discern the pot hanging at the open hearth, and as her eyes adjusted, she could see that Beau was not in the parlor.

She went back into the hallway and peered down a long corridor toward the rear of the house, where utter blackness prevailed. After a moment, forms began to emerge from the darkness. That angular construction at the end of the hall was a staircase, of course. And the shadow on it was surely Beau. He was not climbing the stairs, but stood at the bottom, as if listening. As she stood, watching, she felt the hair on her arms lift in some atavistic warning. She had no idea how she knew, but she suddenly was absolutely certain that she and Beau were not alone in the house. Nor was the other person a friendly one. Some menacing presence lurked nearby. She turned instinctively to flee, then decided she must warn Beau.

Staring toward the staircase, she could not discern any other form. With panic rising to engulf her, she took a sudden dash forward, for she feared that to call her cousin would alert the invisible other and bring disaster down on their heads.

It was about halfway down the long corridor that it happened. One instant she was running, the next instant she had run into a human wall. He must have come out of a doorway leading to the hall. She heard a masculine gasp of surprise, and like an echo, her own lighter gasp following it. Strong hands seized her shoulders. As she stood, trembling in fear for her life, the hands brushed intimately down the sides of her body, gauging her size and sex. Her frightened breaths were the only sound; she was too shocked and afraid even to shout.

Of course, she must call to Beau for help. Even as the thought darted into her mind, the dark head descended and hot lips pressed on hers. Strong arms encircled her waist, crushing her against that firm wall of bone and muscle. Between shock and fear, she scarcely had the strength to struggle.

When she recovered her wits, she braced her hands against the man's shoulders and pushed with all her might, temporarily dislodging him. A low chuckle sounded in her ear, then his arms tightened and he kissed her again, hot and hard and long, as if in punishment for fighting him.

I am ruined! she thought. *This villain is going to have his way with me.*

Then he lifted his head and rubbed his cheek against hers. *"Tu es très méchante, ma chérie,"* he murmured, and was gone as suddenly as he had appeared.

She stood staring all about in the darkness with her heart pounding in painful excitement, forgetful of Beau. A Frenchman! She might have guessed. Only a Frenchie would kiss like that. Shaking herself back to sanity, she looked to the staircase.

Before her gaze had time to focus, she heard a scuffle and a muffled gasp, followed by a dragging sound. The sounds were congruous with a struggle, and someone or something being dragged along the floor. Fear was left behind in her concern for Beau's safety. She moved swiftly forward. Her fear for Beau's life was soon preempted by a fear for her own. Some rough thing — a blanket perhaps — was thrown over her head. It covered her arms and legs, leaving her helpless. She was picked up bodily in a pair of strong arms and carried down the corridor. She heard a door open. She was carried into the room and deposited on the floor. She heard the door close and a key turn.

She immediately pulled the blanket off her head. The stench of fish and seaweed suggested it had been to sea. Before she had time to examine the room she had been placed in, she heard whispers from beyond the door but close at hand. The words sounded like gibberish at first, but as she listened more closely, she could distinguish that it was two men speaking French.

"*J'ai cherché partout. Elle n'est pas ici.*" The man was telling his companion he had looked all over and could not find her — or it. The French had a troublesome habit of ascribing gender to their nouns and pronouns. Was it Dauntry's *chère amie* that was missing?

The reply was also in French. The voice sounded slightly familiar, but the foreign language changed the timbre and inflection beyond recognition. "They must have been looking for it (or possibly her), *non?* We've got to find it/her. I trust you took care of that fellow?"

"Ah, *oui,* and the lady."

"I hope you didn't hurt her?"

"A Frenchman hurt a lady? *Jamais!* Never! I treated her gently as a babe. As to the *gars,* I gave him only a tap on the head."

"*Bon!* I wonder if it" — still that troublesome "*elle,*" for they spoke French — "could be slid under the carpet. Did you look?"

"Under every carpet and in every corner."

The men moved beyond hearing in the corridor, but one thing was now plain — a woman was not hiding under a carpet. Cressida was nearly frightened out of her wits

104

when a hollow voice suddenly spoke from the shadows within the chamber.

"Sid, is that you?"

"Beau! You're alive! Oh, thank God." They both spoke in low voices. "I feared they had killed you." She scrambled out of the blanket and rushed to him. He lay prostrate on the floor, holding his aching head.

"Wounded, not conquered." He struggled to his feet. "Well, this is a fine how-do-you-do. Bested by a pair of Frenchies. Or at least the one who caught me was, to judge by his curses. Took me by surprise, or I would have drawn his cork and darkened his daylights."

"I think it was two Frenchies," she said. Or had one of them been Dauntry? "I don't think they were smugglers, Beau. They were looking for something they called *'elle.'*"

"An ell of smuggled silk," Beau deduced.

"No, not that sort of ell. They were speaking French. It could mean she or it."

"A woman!" Beau exclaimed.

"No, they thought this *elle* might be under a carpet."

"Oh, then it wasn't the lady upstairs they were looking for."

"What lady?"

"I heard light footfalls on the stairs as I went down the corridor. I couldn't see much in the moonlight, but I think I saw a white gown, and light hair. And I know I smelled violet perfume."

"You dreamed it. I saw no lady."

"Of course you didn't. She was hiding — under a carpet for all I know. We've got to help her, Sid."

"You've been reading those gothic novels in the library."

Beau rubbed his head. "You're right, I was having a look at *The Mysterious Warning* this afternoon. Perhaps I dreamed her after I was coshed on the head. But I mean to return — after we escape, I mean — and search the house from top to bottom."

"I shall come with you to search for *elle*. Meanwhile, we must get out of here and follow them, try to overhear what else they say."

"We'd best do it quietly. Follow me." He headed to the door. "Oh, it's locked."

"We shall have to go out by the window." As she spoke, she moved quietly toward the window. The leaded panes that looked so charming from the outside were not made to open. They were firmly held in place by wooden frames with no locks or bolts. Cressida was aware of a sinking sensation in the pit of her stomach. "We are locked in," she said in a dying voice.

Visions of being discovered the next day,

starving and parched from thirst, flashed before her eyes.

"I'll bust the window," Beau said bravely. "But first we'd best listen and make sure they're gone."

Beau put his ear to the door; Cressida looked out the window, which gave an angled view of the rock plateau in front of the cottage and the shining sea below. As she watched, two men came into view around the corner of the cottage. One was in shadow — he might have been Dauntry. But it was at the other that she gazed, a soft smile lifting her lips. Handsome! She felt he was the one who had kissed her and called her naughty. He had a French look about him. All the charm of the French, and the Gallic grace in his shrugging shoulders and gesturing hands. It was difficult to determine his complexion in the wan moonlight, but his hair looked black and his skin swarthy. He was not quite as tall as the other man, and slighter in build, but with broad shoulders.

He tossed up his hands, patted the other man on the shoulder, and walked away, laughing insouciantly. She watched as he clambered like a goat up the rock cliff and disappeared. The other one remained behind, looking uneasily at the cottage. Surely he was not going to go and leave them locked up all night in this horrid house! There might be rats. She peered around the dim corners of the room for signs of vermin. Then, to her great dismay, the second man turned and went down the staircase, away from the cottage.

"They've left," she said to Beau. "Give them five minutes to get beyond earshot, then break a window with a chair, or whatever you can find." They groped about in the darkness for a moment. "Here, this will do for a start," she said when she found a poker by the fireplace.

As she was handing Beau the poker, there was a light rattle at the door. Cressida assumed the man had reconsidered his dastardly first idea of leaving them locked in the house and began considering what excuse she could give for being there. When she heard Muffet's voice, she sighed in relief.

"Missy? Are you in there?"

"Yes! Can you get us out, Muffet?" she called.

The key twisted in the lock and he came into the chamber, tsking and shaking his head.

"What your papa would say about this I do not like to think. Looking at the moon, indeed! I knew you were up to no good."

"Muffet, you are a pearl beyond price,"

she declared, and kissed him on the cheek. "You may lecture me to your heart's content later. Now I want to go home and have a warm bath, for I stink of fish."

"Now, missy, ladies don't use such words as stink. It is not becoming."

"Neither is this stench."

They left the room, Muffet leading, followed by Cressida, and Beau with the poker bringing up the rear.

"I shall just check up on the lady in white," Beau said, and went to the bottom of the stairs. "Is there anyone up there?" he called. "They're gone. You can come down if you're there. We shan't harm you. We're friends." He waited, and called again, then ran up to the top of the stairs and opened every bedroom door, but seeing no one, he returned below.

"Wishful thinking," he said sheepishly, and they went out into the moonlit night.

Dauntry watched them from behind a concealing hedge. He had seen Muffet coming and was relieved that he did not have to confront Cressida after his partner had locked her up in that room. Not that she didn't deserve it! A smile quirked his lips. Perhaps this interlude would dampen her enthusiasm for the cottage. If the incarceration didn't do it, the kiss surely would.

He was fairly sure she had not found the letter, at least. She had been inside for only a minute before she was intercepted.

He was beginning to realize hers was not a spirit to be quenched by a mere fright in a dark house. He must arrange some more daunting obstacle to her returning, and he had a fair idea what would keep her away. He would bring some fair charmer down from London and install her in the cottage for the next few weeks. Amarylla was at leisure since the closing of her latest play. If she had not taken a new patron yet, she would do admirably.

Cressida peered all around before leaving. Seeing the coast was clear, the trio hastened along the beach, back to the dower house. It was Beau who stopped and looked back at the cottage before they rounded the bend in the coast that cut it off from view. He was hoping to see a head at a window, but he saw only the reflected moonlight. They picked up their pace and soon reached home. Miss Wantage had not been asking for them, as Cressida feared she might, but Jennet soon appeared at the saloon door to inquire what Miss Wantage meant by a Welsh posset, which she had asked for.

"Heated milk and vanilla, and three teaspoons of sugar with nutmeg grated on top," Cressida replied.

"Oh, you mean a spinster's nightcap. Why didn't she say so?"

At this saucy speech, Cressida had to remind herself poor Jennet's brain was addled and did not scold her.

"And a regular posset for her ladyship," Muffet told Jennet. "Which you will take up to bed with you, missy."

He was not such an optimist as to expect he would be obeyed, nor was he. Cressida and Beau sat for close to an hour discussing their adventure, and what steps they could take to discover *elle*.

"I wonder if it's brandy they're hiding in that cottage," Beau said, his brow puckered in concentration. "It's *l'eau de vie* in French — feminine, *elle*."

"It would not be easy to lose a cargo of brandy in that little chalet. No, it's something small enough to hide under a carpet. A paper? No, that's masculine, *le papier*. A letter, perhaps. That's feminine."

"I believe you've got it. We must get into the house in daylight," Beau said. "One of us will stand guard while t'other goes in and has a look around. First light tomorrow we shall go, before Dauntry is up and about."

"Excellent thinking, Beau. Next time we

shall go by daylight, and take a pistol, if you have one."

"I always carry one in the side pocket when I travel. Well, shall we hit the tick, then? I fancy I shall dream of the mysterious lady in white."

Cressida just smiled. She knew what she would dream of. The dashing Frenchman who had kissed her in the dark and called her *chérie*. It had been a very nice kiss. Overpowering, but not roughly so. He could have harmed her had he wished. But he only kissed her, rather playfully really, as if demanding a forfeit for her transgression into his business. Perhaps they would see him tomorrow at the chalet. . . .

Chapter Eight

Cressida awoke in the morning with a sense of tingling excitement. The ennui of isolation had been blown away by the interlude at the cottage. Now that she had a mystery — and a dashing Frenchman — to amuse her, she did not bother posting her letter inviting her friends to call. Beau was in a similar mood.

"I dreamed of her last night," he said with a wobbly smile. "I have already been past the cottage once. I think I saw a movement in one of the attic windows, but I could not be sure. I have been thinking about Jennet's taking a tray to the cottage yesterday. She might have been taking it to the lady in white, eh?" he said.

"I begin to think there really was a lady in white, although I did not see her. Tory is up to anything."

"True, she could teach the Jesuits a thing or two about ratiocination." When Cressida frowned at this heavy word, he translated it for her. "Reasoning," he said.

"I'm glad to learn your expensive education was not entirely wasted."

"Devil a bit of it. I had a lovely time at Oxford. When I go to the cottage this morning, I mean to do a thorough search. I only peeked into the bedrooms last night. The lady might have been hiding in a clothespress or some such thing."

"What will you do if you find her, Beau?" she asked, just making conversation. The question of more interest to her was what would she do if she met her handsome Frenchman? He was no rough smuggler; he had been wearing a well-tailored superfine jacket. Probably one of the aristos who had sought safety in England during the revolution in France. One occasionally came across them in London. And there was no stigma attached to marrying one. . . .

Cressida was too impatient to make a proper breakfast. She nibbled idly on a piece of toast and sipped a cup of coffee. As soon as she put her cup down, Beau was on his feet.

"Shall we go? I have my pistol right here." He patted a bulge under his jacket.

"I wore my riding habit to fool Muffet. We shall leave by the back door; he'll think we are going to the stable," she replied. It was her newest, most fashionable habit that she wore, the burgundy one. Before leaving, she perched her hat over her eye and caught it under the chin with a ribbon. The winds were strong by the sea.

They skirted around the rear of the house and clambered down to the beach beyond a sight of the dower house. The cottage, perched on the cliff, looked innocent in daylight, with the windows reflecting a golden sun instead of pale moonlight. No lady appeared at any of the windows.

"We shall knock at the door like regular visitors," Beau said. "If there's no answer, we'll go in. The door was not locked last night."

They did as he suggested. Three rattles of the brass knocker brought no reply. Beau tried the doorknob. "It's locked!" he said. "We left it on the latch last night when we left. Someone is here right enough. Shall I knock the door down?"

"Let us try the back door. And, Beau, best have your pistol ready."

The path to the rear was overgrown, not with poison ivy or poison oak, but with harmless English ivy that formed a green carpet over the stone and clambered up toward the land above. The back door was reached by a set of wooden steps. As they mounted the stairs, Cressida gave a little shriek.

There, just outside the back door, sat a

silver tea tray, the same one she was accustomed to having her tea served on. On the tray sat a teapot and Wedgwood dishes, still holding the remains of a breakfast. Only one of the boiled eggs had been eaten. The other was still in its cup. A piece of toast had one bite out of it. A covered silver jam pot was there as well, along with a discarded linen napkin.

"These dishes are from the dower house!" she exclaimed, staring in confusion.

Beau paid her no heed. "I was right!" he said exultantly. "She is here. We must rescue her."

"I am not sure she wants rescuing! It seems to me she is living in luxury — at my expense. My servants must be bringing these meals from my kitchen. How dare he!"

"Who?" Beau asked in confusion.

"The so-called lady you saw last night is no one else but Dauntry's *chère amie.* She ran up to the attic when the Frenchies broke into the house. He as well as told me he had a woman here, and I, like a fool, did not believe him."

"It seems to me you are jumping to conclusions," Beau said. He was reluctant to give up his romantic dream.

"We'll see about that. I shall call on him at once."

"It might be best to wait until he calls. I mean to say — Lady Dauntry. Not the thing to bring the dirty linen into her saloon."

"You are right. I shall send a note demanding that he call on me. He must come at once, for he mentioned leaving for London today. We shall not honor his *chère amie* with a morning call, Beau."

"Shall I take the tray?"

"No, leave the evidence here. I want to confront him with it."

She turned and strode clown the stairs without so much as a backward glance.

"But what about the lady?" Beau asked. "I think I ought to try to rescue her." He tried the door, but it was locked

"Rescue a lightskirt from one of the richest patrons in England? I doubt she will thank you for that, but if you want to make a cake of yourself, go ahead," she called back without breaking stride.

Beau ran after her, arguing and trying to convince himself the woman was being kept there under duress.

"Don't be an ass, Beau," she said sharply. "You saw Jennet leaving the house with a tray yesterday. She was obviously bringing it here. If Dauntry's woman cannot overpower or outwit that simple girl, then she does not deserve rescuing. She is obviously here by choice."

"I daresay you are right," he finally admitted.

They returned by the shortest route, the beach. Beau spent no time at the dower house that morning. He spotted the *Sea Dog* sailing around the outcropping a mile off Beachy Head and was in the house only long enough to pick up his telescope to watch her progress. In his excitement, he forgot all about the mysterious lady in white.

Cressida wrote a brief, angry note to the castle, asking if Dauntry would please call on a most urgent matter before leaving for London. While awaiting his arrival, she rang for Tory, who came puffing into the saloon.

"What can I do for you, milady?" she asked with an ingratiating smile.

"You can stop sending Jennet to the cottage with trays from my kitchen," she said.

"Ah, the trays. You see, it is like this. Jennet is a bit of a knock-in-the-cradle, as you well know."

"I am aware of that, Mrs. Armstrong. I, on the other hand, have the full use of my wits. Pray do not try to con me with one of your stories. Jennet does not take my good silver and china to eat her meals on the door stoop of the chalet, where I discovered them

118

this morning. I know the meals are going to Dauntry's — friend. You are taking your orders from me now, not Lord Dauntry. Is that quite clear?"

"As clear as a bell, milady. Just as you say. No more trays." Strangely, Mrs. Armstrong looked relieved.

Cressida took pity on her. "I do not hold you entirely accountable, Tory," she said more gently. "Old habits die hard, and I know you are accustomed to taking orders from Dauntry."

"He cuts up rusty if you don't do just as he says."

"Let him send trays from the castle if he has no cook for her."

"Now, there is an idea!" Tory exclaimed, smiling.

"I wonder it did not occur to him in the first place. It is because the dower house is so much closer, I expect."

"That's it exactly. Would you care to give me the menu for dinner while I am here? Them steps . . ." She drew a weary sigh and wiped imaginary perspiration from her forehead.

"It doesn't matter. I am not in a mood to discuss it. Some pork might be nice for a change."

"Ah, now, there is a pity, for there isn't an

ounce of pork in the larder. I've a nice joint of beef."

"Very well, with some peas."

Why did the woman bother to consult her if the decisions were already taken? "Tomorrow we shall have a roast of pork."

"Certainly, milady. I'll make you up a nice prune sauce to go with it, from Cook's receipt at the castle."

"Thank you. That will be all for now."

"Then I'll just see to Miss Wantage's tray, for she claims she is ailing again, though she asked for two eggs and gammon for breakfast. Cleaned her platter, too. She says she will be down for lunch. She wants pork jelly, if you please, and me with not a drop of pork in the house."

"Beef jelly will do."

"It will have to. What ails the lady, if you don't mind my asking?"

With no sensible reply, Cressida said, "She has a nervous disorder."

"Ah, one of *them!*"

Tory disappeared in a bustle of starched apron. Cressida sat on, tapping her toe and glancing at the clock. When a half hour's wait did not bring Dauntry, she could sit still no longer and saddled up her mare to go after him. She would not mention the matter in front of his mama, but she would have this out with him before he left.

At the castle Dauntry sat musing over her note as he sipped his morning coffee. The imperious tone of it annoyed him to no small degree. He was strongly inclined to ignore Cressida's summons, but curiosity impelled him toward the dower house. What would she say about last night? Had she recognized him? That was the obvious reason for this curt note. Yet he was sure she could not have positively identified him. He had spoken French — it changed the quality of the voice, and in the darkness she could not have gotten a good look at him. He would play dumb, display utter astonishment at her story just before delivering her a thumping lecture for having trespassed against his express orders. It was Lady deCourcy who was in the wrong here, and he would let her know it.

He called for his bay gelding and rode off toward the dower house. He met Cressida just past the turnoff to the cottage. Each recognized in the stiff pose of the other the signs of anger and intransigence. Yet despite his temper, Dauntry observed how gracefully she sat her recount, how at home she looked in the saddle. He admired a good horsewoman. He also admired the jaunty angle of her curled beaver. Her beauty lent a fillip to the coming confrontation.

"Good morning, Lady deCourcy," Dauntry said coolly. "You wished a word with me?"

"I should like an explanation of why you are entertaining your company at my expense, sir."

He hardly knew what she would say, but this assertion caught him off guard. "What the devil are you talking about?" he asked in confusion.

"I am talking about the woman in the chalet. Shabby treatment of a *chère amie*, Dauntry. If you cannot control your — appetite, I suggest you do the thing up properly and hire her some servants, for she will no longer have the use of my kitchen and servants."

His brow furrowed in consternation. "Woman? What woman? I don't know what you're talking about."

"You admitted you have a woman there."

"I said the cottage is used from time to time. It has stood empty the past two years. Amary — my friend — should be arriving soon, as a matter of fact. Are you saying there is already a woman there?"

Angry and confused as she was, Cressida still found a few seconds to conjure with that "Amary —" When had Dauntry taken that high flyer Amarylla under his protection? She had heard nothing of it in London.

"Certainly there is. Come along and I shall show you."

They cantered down the road to the chalet without exchanging another word. Although Cressida was now convinced it was not Dauntry who was making use of her kitchen and staff, she was still out of reason cross with him. If the cottage had been unoccupied, he could have let her have it. Why did he bother bringing a mistress here at all, when he spent most of his time in town? Was the man a satyr? A gentleman of his age ought to be married and setting up his nursery. He gave a bad example to the younger bachelors.

They dismounted at the dower house and walked along the beach, up the stairs to the cottage, and around to the rear door. Cressida stopped a moment to point at the ivy, saying, "This, for your information, Dauntry, is not poison ivy, but plain old English ivy."

Wrapped in conjecture, he did not reply.

When she climbed the stairs at the back door, Cressida saw the tray was gone. That, too, annoyed her. She looked a fool. "It was here this morning. Someone has removed it," she said.

"May I know what you were doing here,

trespassing on my property earlier this morning?" Dauntry asked, a black brow lifting arrogantly. "I specifically told you it was out of bounds."

"We were walking on the beach and — stopped to have a look about."

"At the back door. I see. Well, we must get to the bottom of this. I won't have trespassers. Tory, I suppose, is the culprit."

"But Tory said you —" She came to a pause. "Actually, she did not say you had told her to bring the trays, but when I said it, she let me believe it." As she had let her believe Melbury was Mr. Brewster.

"I was the suspect from the beginning, was I?" he asked with something between a smile and a sneer.

"It is your house after all."

"You would do well to remember it in future."

"Never mind mounting your high horse, Dauntry. I admit I had no business here, but neither had my silver tray. Who could be here?"

"There is one way to find out."

He took a key ring from his pocket, inserted a key in the lock, and opened the door. The house, though sound in structure, showed an air of dereliction by daylight. The curtains were fatigued and faded, the furniture dusty, and the air smelled of seaweed. Cressida was aware of how much finer and more comfortable the dower house was. She wondered that Dauntry would install such an Incomparable as Amarylla here.

As they went from room to room, small signs of recent occupancy were spotted, but a search of the house from kitchen to attic produced no one. There was a wineglass on a table in the saloon and a pitcher of water in one of the bedrooms. Only one bed was made up with linen. It had been slept in and not remade.

As they toured, Cressida observed that Dauntry was examining unlikely spots for a visitor to have left traces. He looked in drawers and shook out books, as if looking for a paper of some sort — the missing letter, no doubt. Was it possible Dauntry had been the other man at the chalet last night? The man was about his size, and Dauntry had been heading this way when he left the dower house. What business would he have with a Frenchie? Smuggling, very likely. She could not believe it was anything worse; spying, for instance. His character was good.

In the study, the same one where Cressida and Beau had been incarcerated the night before, although nothing was said of that, they found a cigar butt in a saucer.

"A man was here!" Cressida exclaimed.

Dauntry's frown dwindled to resignation. "Cousin Melbury," he said. "I warrant he arranged with the servants to spend the night here when he called on you yesterday, and even convinced them to feed him. I shall have a word with Tory."

"How would he have gotten in? There are no windows broken."

"He must have snitched the spare key the last time he was in my study — or bribed one of my servants to get it for him. He is a formidable wheedler. And, of course, the servants have known him forever. They watched him grow up."

"I would say he still has a deal of growing up to do."

"Of course, but the ladies are always eager to oblige a handsome, charming rogue."

Cressida stared. "I did not find him so handsome as all that. As to charming, his brash swaggering is not my idea of charm."

Dauntry cast a sideways glance at her. "You have higher standards than I would have expected from your encouragement of the duke," he murmured.

"I did not encourage the duke in the least."

"Indeed? I had not thought the baroness would allow herself to be put upon by anyone. If you wished to discourage him, you could have done it, and put the poor fellow out of his misery." And she could have discouraged Saintbury, too, instead of breaking his heart.

"Oh, but he enjoys his misery. It is half an act with him."

"And it is all an act with you," he riposted.

"Are you attempting, in your clumsy way, to read me a lecture, Dauntry?" she inquired in a thin voice.

"A word to the wise, my dear. You are picking up the aroma of a flirt."

She flounced across the room, peering for further signs of occupancy, and found a glass holding an inch of ale in the bottom. Ladies seldom drank ale. She showed it to Dauntry. "Definitely a man," she said, "and Tory let me believe it was a woman!"

Dauntry examined her with a dark eye. "You found it easy to believe she was my bit o' muslin, eh?"

"Oh, no, Dauntry," she said with a quizzing smile. "I was shocked with you. I made sure your women would be kept in a much grander style. Amarylla will not be content without a full staff of servants to bring this place into order. She will require a carriage. She is accustomed to the best. I had not heard Everly had tired of her charms."

Dauntry was not so well up on gossip as

Cressida. He had not heard Everly was involved with the actress. "She tired of his, actually," he said.

"I wish you luck of your bargain. She is monstrously expensive, from what I hear."

"And worth every penny. Let us go."

Tory was soon standing before them, clutching at her apron skirts and bursting into a frenzy of apologies. "I'm ever so sorry, your lordship. I expect I done wrong to let her ladyship think it was your friend that was eating the food, but when she suggested it, I leapt on it to protect Melbury. You know how Melbury is. He could work his way around a heart of stone." She turned to Cressida. "Sure it was only a bit of gingerbread and bacon and eggs, milady. I did not think you would begrudge it to a starving man."

"I do not begrudge it, Tory, but you should have told me."

"Where has he gone?" Dauntry asked.

"I sent the footman to warn him the jig was up," Tory admitted shamelessly. "He mentioned Bath."

"Good riddance. If he shows up at the door again, send him to me."

"I will, your lordship. I'm sorry, milady. I sent off to the castle for the pork jelly for Miss Wantage, as the poor creature is such a bundle of nerves." She curtsied and backed toward the doorway.

Cressida's cheeks felt warm at this speech. "Be sure you pay the cook for it, Tory," she said. "I will not be pillaging Dauntry's kitchen."

"You can just give me the penny while I am here," he said, chewing back a grin.

Tory left. "Don't let me keep you, Dauntry," Cressida said. "No doubt you are eager to be off to London to collect Amarylla."

"I changed my mind." Cressida felt a rush of triumph. No, *she* had changed his mind, but he was too proud to say so.

"I shall send my groom off for her. I must remain here and get the cottage ready for her. As you so kindly pointed out, it is in no shape for company."

Her eyes sparked angrily. "Don't let me keep you from your dissipations," she said, and flounced out of the room.

Chapter Nine

That afternoon Cressida received an invitation from Lady Dauntry inviting her household to an informal dinner at the castle that evening. She promised it would be a small, quiet do, in keeping with the baroness's rustication. It made a pleasant diversion, as Beau was no longer available for company. Since the arrival of his yacht, she had scarcely seen him. He did not even come to the house for lunch, causing grim forecasts of sunstroke, starvation, and, of course, eventual drowning from Miss Wantage.

Cressida drove Miss Wantage into the village in the afternoon to exchange the vulgar silk threads for pastel ones. Miss Wantage could happily have spent the whole day in the drapery shop, comparing prices and quality, and pointing out to Cressida that Mrs. Flynn, whom Cressida had never heard of, had a gown made of that blue mulled muslin last year and it had faded shockingly.

"They are asking nine shillings the yard!" she exclaimed. "I am sure Mrs. Flynn paid only six — and well paid for it was at that price. It is not real Indian muslin," she said, holding an end up to the light to check the closeness of the weave and the density of the threads.

"The embroidery supplies are over here," Cressida said, trying to nudge her in the proper direction.

"Just look at this, Cressida!" was Miss Wantage's reply. "The Indian muslin is fifteen shillings the yard! Did you ever hear of such a thing? Plain old muslin. Mind you, the green sprigged pattern is pretty. They do not carry the green sprigged in Bath."

"Would you like a few yards, Miss Wantage?" Cressida asked. Perhaps that was why she lingered so long over the ells.

"I would not be caught dead in it at my age. We aging ladies must be a little careful what colors we wear." Her eyes just glanced off Cressida's pink sprigged muslin. "Mutton dressed as lamb, as my papa was used to say. If I were buying any material, I would buy a good merino for a winter suit. Not that I am hinting!"

Her pale fingers moved over to the winter materials, landing on a bolt of gray merino (at a guinea a yard). After much discussion, Miss Wantage was prevailed upon to take four yards as a gift. "And the extra half yard for errors," she added. "One never knows, a sleeve might be cut wrong, and then where are you, with the source of the material miles away in Beachy Head?"

They moved on to the buttons (common), lace (that lot never came out of Belgium!), and needles. The worst to be said of them was that the eyes were too small. Finally they reached the embroidery threads, only to discover that Miss Wantage had "accidentally" left the vulgar bright ones at home, which did not prevent her from snapping up the pastel shades. A full hour later they left the shop to find the sky had darkened during their sojourn amid the sewing materials.

Miss Wantage shook her head. "I hope Beau has the sense to come in out of the rain, but I doubt it."

It had begun sprinkling by the time they reached home, giving great pleasure to Miss Wantage, who had insisted on the closed carriage. Beau's yacht was seen a mile out at sea, but as the wind was not strong, Cressida could not be convinced to either fear for his life or send a rescue ship out after him. At six Beau came bouncing into the saloon, his face ruddy and his hair looking like a haystack.

"By Jove, this is something like! Nick let me work the rudder. I brought us into harbor with a little help from Nick and the crew."

"Who is Nick?" Miss Wantage inquired, for she mistrusted this name of ill omen.

"My captain, Nick Bolton. An excellent fellow. He sailed under Nelson, until he had his arm shot off. Nelson, I mean. Nick still has both of his." He looked at the puddle of gray merino in Miss Wantage's lap and said, "I say, has someone died?"

Miss Wantage cast a sad eye on him. "One ought not to make jokes about death, Beau. It is coming to us all, sooner or later."

"I wasn't joking."

"It is time to dress for dinner," Cressida said. "We are invited to the castle, Beau."

"I hope they have invited some ladies. The neighborhood is thin of ladies. I have not seen a pretty face since I arrived."

It had been understood when Miss Wantage was taken on that she would perform as Cressida's dresser. Until the present, her poor health had prevented it. She made a token offer now.

"Would you like me to try to do something with your hair, dear?" she said, looking uncertainly at Cressida's raven tousle of curls. "The sea air is so hard on it, is it not? I really don't know what could be done with it. A turban, perhaps."

"I look a quiz in a turban."

"I agree, it takes a well-proportioned face

to do justice to a turban. I have a few spare caps with me, if you would like to borrow one."

Cressida refused to take issue on the caps. "Jennet usually helps me dress."

"Oh, the simpleton. That accounts for it," Miss Wantage said, and walked languidly up to her room.

Beau grinned. "Now that Jeremiah has completely demoralized you, I want to say that I think your hair looks dashed nice, Sid. How do you keep your patience with that creature?"

"I try not to listen, but on this occasion I have been amusing myself by wondering how Dauntry will take to her slights. He was quick to condemn us for speaking ill of Miss Wantage. Let us see how much forbearance he has."

"She'll not blister him with that tongue of hers. She likes a marquess very well. He comes right below a duke. If she tries her stunts on him, he will give her a set-down in short order."

Cressida's mirror told her that her hair looked fine. She had Jennet brush it out and pinned a pearl brooch in the curls above her left ear. For a simple country party, she wore a crepe gown in pale green with a simple strand of pearls. Jennet brought her a perfect white rosebud, which she pinned at her bodice.

"Oh, so you are wearing that. It is no matter. No one will see us," was Miss Wantage's forgiving speech when Cressida entered the saloon.

Lady Dauntry delayed dinner until eight for her party, but her guests began arriving at seven. The party from the dower house arrived at seven-thirty, to find the saloon well populated. Allan Brewster and his parents were there, as were the vicar and his wife and a sprinkling of country neighbors. Lady Dauntry introduced Lady deCourcy's party to them. If Beau found the few young ladies present objectionable, one would never have guessed it from the way he went haring after them.

Lord Dauntry was present to play host. He was on good terms with his neighbors. The gentlemen spoke of farming and politics while the ladies caught up on the local gossip over a glass of sherry. Miss Wantage requested water.

"Have you heard from the honeymooners, Lady Dauntry?" Mrs. Simmons, the vicar's wife, inquired.

"Not a word! I expected Tony would write from Haslemere, where they were to rest the first day after the wedding."

"They have better things to do, hee-hee," the vicar said.

Miss Wantage stiffened. "Indeed they would have," she said. "There is a fine church there, if memory serves."

The talk turned to other neighbors, finally hitting on another name Cressida recognized, James Melbury.

"I hear Melbury is off to Bath, Lady Dauntry," a Mrs. Forrester said.

"I believe he mentioned something of the sort at the wedding."

"Yes," Mrs. Forrester continued, "the Anglins saw him at the Assembly Rooms there the night before last, chasing after Miss Addams."

Dinner was soon called. Cressida had the place of honor at Lord Dauntry's right side. She said in a low voice, "Melbury was seen at Bath the night before last. He could not possibly have been home by yesterday, when that man visited me, could he?"

"Only if he rode *ventre à terre,* which suggests someone was after him. That is not uncommon."

"He could scarcely do it, even on horseback. Is it possible my caller and the man who was staying at the cottage is not Melbury?"

I have been wondering the same thing.

Brewster tells me Melbury did not attend the assembly in Peachy Head this week. If he were in the neighborhood, he would no more miss an assembly than he'd fail to show up on quarter day with his palm out. We must speak of this in private later."

Although the dinner was only for a few country neighbors, it was conducted in an elegant manner, with several courses and removes. Miss Wantage had escaped the turbot in white sauce at the dower house, only to find it waiting for her at the castle, but as she said to Cressida later, "At least the sauce was not full of lumps."

What she was saying to her neighbors could not be heard from the head of the table, but their glum faces told Cressida she was in her usual Job-like mood, scattering gloom in all directions. As a kindness to the rest of the company, Cressida sat beside her in the saloon after dinner, while awaiting the gentlemen. Lady Dauntry, who treated her noble guest with great consideration, shared the sofa.

"Did I hear you say you are from Bath, Miss Wantage?" she asked.

"I spend the winter months there with my cousin."

"Not as an invalid, I hope?"

"At my age, madame, one cannot expect good health."

"Why, you are young!" Lady Dauntry exclaimed. "I could give you a decade, and I do not call myself old."

"Yet your liver gives you considerable grief, I think?" Miss Wantage said, examining the lady's complexion. "That sallow tinge to the skin usually indicates a bad liver. And those mottled marks on your hands. My aunt Agnes had sunk into such a complexion just before she passed on."

Lady Dauntry looked at her hands in dismay. "Wine, of course, is slow death," Miss Wantage continued. "Not to speak out of turn, but I noticed you emptied not less than three wineglasses at dinner, and two of sherry before you sat down. I take only water. A pity you could not get to Bath. The waters there would do wonders for your condition. I could recommend an excellent doctor. He handles all the elderly ladies."

Lady Dauntry soon rose, saying she must just speak to Mrs. Brewster. She cast a glance of deepest sympathy on the baroness as she went.

Before long, the gentlemen arrived from the dining room, smelling of port and cigars. Dauntry would not satisfy Cressida to dart to her side. He stopped for a word with Mrs.

138

Simmons, but was soon working his way to the empty chair beside Lady deCourcy and her companion.

"Miss Wantage," he said, "although I have been to the dower house a few times, I have not had much opportunity to become acquainted with you. How are you liking the seaside?" He sat down.

"I can understand now why all your neighbors have such rough complexions," was her reply. "It is the salty wind that accounts for it."

He made an effort to turn this unpromising opening into a compliment. "It must be the more clement air of Bath that accounts for your own youthful color," he said.

Marquess or no, she did not let him get away with implying she was in good health. "I am flushed. I am not accustomed to taking such a heavy dinner. A little gruel or bread and milk satisfies me. Much healthier."

"Feeling peaked, are you? Let me get you a glass of wine."

"Wine!" she said as if he had offered her hemlock. "There has been more than enough wine served. I would appreciate a glass of water, if it is not too much trouble."

Dauntry lifted his finger, and his butler came to receive his order. He was back in a minute with a glass of water.

"What a very odd taste the water has here," Miss Wantage said after sipping it. "I wonder if it is the salt from the sea seeping into the ground water, or rotten fish that accounts for it."

"I shall ask Eaton to get you a fresh glass," Dauntry said, his patience growing thin.

"Oh, pray, do not bother about me. The water at the dower house is the same — unpotable. I have asked Mrs. Armstrong to boil it before serving, but I doubt she does it. She is an irascible old lady. You were wise to palm her off on Lady deCourcy, milord. She must be a scourge to your dear mama, but of course, one cannot turn off old retainers. It would be unchristian."

"I insist on getting you fresh water," he said, using it for an excuse to leave.

"Dauntry seems very agreeable," Miss Wantage said to Cressida when they were alone. "Breeding will always tell. A marquess. Pity he could not take a liking to you, but I noticed he hardly glanced at you the whole time he was here. A very obliging gentleman."

Vicar Simmons had not sat beside Miss Wantage at dinner, and thus did not know what he was getting into when he joined her and Lady deCourcy. Cressida left at once, using the excuse of meeting the neighbors.

She had a word with Brewster, who was concerned at learning Melbury had been spotted in Bath.

"You cannot think of anyone else it might have been?" she asked.

"It could have been some wandering thief reconnoitering the house to rob it. You want to make sure you lock up your doors at night."

"But how did he know your name? And he seemed familiar with the family and house as well — and the servants."

"P'raps Melbury coached someone."

Dauntry did not take Miss Wantage her fresh water in person. He had Eaton deliver it. Miss Wantage took one sip, screwed up her face, and set it aside. Even Eaton, that perfect model of a butler, allowed a flash of impatience to darken his brow.

Before long, Dauntry worked his way over to Brewster and Lady deCourcy.

"Dashed odd about Melbury," Brewster said to him. "We were just discussing it. It cannot have been him who visited the baroness using my name. Does he have any other cousins who look something like him?"

"The family is large. It is possible," Dauntry said.

"Brewster thinks the man might be conniving with Melbury in a break-in," Cressida said. Naturally, this was a concern, the more so as the valuables in the house were not her own.

"I shouldn't think so," Dauntry said. "I would have heard if Melbury had turned ken smasher. In that unlikely event, it would be the castle he invaded. There is not much worth stealing at the dower house."

"There is the silver plate, and my jewelry," she pointed out. "I brought some of my smaller pieces with me."

"Leave them in my safe here if you are concerned," he offered.

"That is not very convenient."

Brewster wandered off to join Beau. Before long, they were deep in nautical terms, vis-à-vis the *Sea Dog* and Brewster's *Stella Maris*.

Dauntry wore such a serious face that Cressida thought he was concerned about Melbury, but when he spoke, it was about something else entirely.

"I owe you an apology, Lady deCourcy, and compliments."

"What have I done now?" she asked, scurrying around in her mind to find the sting in his words.

He shook his head. "You did not hit me over the head with the poker when I read you that presumptuous lecture on the manner in which you and Beau spoke of your companion. Now that I know her, I can only wonder at your forbearance."

"Why, you have not heard anything yet. She likes you. She thinks you are an extremely obliging fellow. Ask your mama what she thinks of her."

"It is not necessary. I met Mama in the hall. We were both begging Eaton to fetch us a headache powder. Mama plans to call her doctor tomorrow to get a diet for her liver. How do you put up with that woman?"

"It is only for three months. The family shares the trial. That is what families are for. You have that scapegrace Melbury. I have an active member of the Clapham sect."

"I know which I would prefer! I was certainly wrong about you. I thought you were a spoiled beauty, but I see you are nothing less than a saint — as well as the best horsewoman in England."

"I do not claim to be the best horsewoman in England, or even in London. Lettie Lade outshines me. My hands and arms lack the strength to handle a team of four, as she does."

"There was gossip of another pending engagement last spring, I believe — Lord Saintbury . . ."

"He did offer. I liked him, but . . . It was

my first Season, although I was older than the other debs. I could not like to accept an offer so soon, for I had no experience with such lively doings as a London Season. It seemed like a dream. I kept thinking that if I accepted Saintbury, I would have to go to live in Somerset with him, and I could not bear to think of giving up all the balls and parties and concerts and plays. We lived in a very retired manner at home. Papa was an invalid for several years. I attended a few small local parties, but was never allowed to have one at home. I was a regular greenhorn when I first went to London, Dauntry. When Saintbury asked me to marry him, I asked for a week to think it over, for I was very fond of him, you know. I believe he took it for mere coyness on my part, but it was not that. Such an important decision should be carefully considered. It would not be fair to him or me to marry him if I was not sure I loved him. And it seems I did not, for I soon forgot all about him."

Dauntry listened and found himself reassessing his opinion of Lady deCourcy. She had taken London by storm; what he had not considered was that her first Season had also taken her by storm. Her age had suggested broad experience in society, but in fact she was a greenhorn, as she had said.

What had seemed like pertness bordering on brashness to society had been country manners, unpolished by contact with the ton.

"Saintbury recovered," he said. He found it easy to forgive her for not rushing into marriage with the first man she found congenial. As he considered it, he thought Saintbury had tried to rush her into an engagement too quickly.

Lady Dauntry appeared at their side and said, "Some of the youngsters are going to dance in the ballroom, if you would like to join them, Lady deCourcy, but I believe your companion wishes to return home."

Cressida first looked eager, but when Miss Wantage was mentioned, her enthusiasm faded. "I had best go with her," she said. "She will not like to drive home alone in the carriage."

"Let Montgomery take her," Dauntry said, and strode off to enlist Beau's help.

Cressida went to bid Miss Wantage adieu. "Tory will attend to your posset. I shan't be late, Miss Wantage, but don't wait up."

"I never can sleep until all the house is tucked into their beds," she replied, "for I feel the responsibility of my position."

Dauntry recognized this velvet-gloved tyranny for what it was and said, "I recommend a strong dose of laudanum." Putting his hand

145

under Cressida's elbow, he led her off to the ballroom. "She spoiled dinner; I'll be damned if I'll let her spoil the dancing," he said grimly. "Her concern is only tyranny disguised as responsibility."

"She does have trouble sleeping."

"Why don't you hire someone to knock her over the head with a poker?" he said brusquely.

Chapter Ten

In the ballroom, the piano player and fiddler were tuning up for a rowdy country dance. Dauntry looked questioningly at Cressida, who was peering at him in the same uncertain manner.

"Shall we wait for a waltz?" he said.

"If you like," was her unhelpful reply.

"In that charming gown — and the skirt is rather narrow."

"It is plenty wide enough. If you are too toplofty to join in the country dance, Dauntry, do not put it in my dish. I shall stand up with Mr. Brewster."

When she turned to step away, Dauntry's hand clasped her wrist and spun her back. She noticed his eyes wore a different expression, a gleam of slumbering fire. His lips were curved in an anticipatory way. She thought of the old adage, "Let sleeping dogs lie." What had she awoken in Dauntry?

"Toplofty?" he asked. "I was merely trying to anticipate what would please you."

"Like Miss Wantage," she said with a quizzing grin.

"Wretch!" His fingers tightened on her wrist, then slid down to grip her fingers possessively as he led her to join the line of dancers.

Both country born and bred, they enjoyed the rowdy romp as much as their neighbors. In fact, Dauntry had not so enjoyed himself in a purely physical way since taking his seat in the House and setting up as a man-about-town. He felt youthful again as his body moved to the beat of the piano and the flying notes of the fiddle. He knew the cause of the pleasure was not mere physical exertion, but the letting down of barriers between himself and Cressida. They felt and behaved like adolescents. He had seen her perform in this manner before and had thought the worse of her for it, branding her a hoyden. What a priggish ass he had become! When the dance finished, their faces were flushed and their toilettes disarranged.

"We have earned a glass of wine," Dauntry decreed.

Cressida glanced at herself in the mirror. "I should tidy myself up. I look as if I had just run a three-legged race." The glowing eyes smiling back at her in the mirror looked as if she had not only run the race, but won it.

"A good thing your chaperon will be in bed when you return," he replied, familiarly tucking a stray curl behind her ear. "Those pious females, always hawking after signs of lechery, put the worst possible construction on innocent doings."

"I blame it on an overdose of Hannah More," she said, reaching to straighten his cravat, which had worked loose.

Dauntry found no fault in her unbuttoned behavior on this occasion. In fact, he felt an unexpected thrill when she touched him in that intimate way, like a wife putting the final touch on her husband's toilette before sending him into the world. " 'An old bishop in petticoats,' Cobbett called Hannah More," he said distractedly.

"We are being quite horrid, Dauntry. Let us not speak ill of the absent."

"You are right, as usual. There are plenty of the present company for us to disparage."

She slapped his hand playfully. "Why is it so delightful to make fun of people behind their backs? It makes us feel superior, I suppose. I need a glass of wine before I die of thirst. And none of that salty, fishy water, mind."

Refreshments had been set up in the morning parlor, where other thirsty dancers milled about the table. Without speaking, but as if

149

reading each other's minds, Cressida and Dauntry turned to leave the room as soon as they picked up a glass of wine. Peering into the saloon, they saw Lady Dauntry had had a few card tables set up, thus robbing them of privacy there. They continued walking along the long marble corridor.

"You are not at all what I thought you would be like," Cressida said. "In London, you always looked as if you were scowling at me. I took the notion you disliked me."

"How could I dislike you? I scarcely knew you, except by reputation."

A shadow appeared in her eyes. "Do I have a horrid reputation, Dauntry? I know I sometimes break society's rules, but I do not do it on purpose. If you say what you are thinking, or do what seems natural, people seem to find it odd. No one told me you had to have the patroness's permission to waltz at Almack's. How should I think of asking permission, when all the younger debs were waltzing?"

"A tempest in a teapot," he said forgivingly, though that was not what he had said at the time. He had agreed with Lady Jersey that Lady deCourcy was a hurly-burly girl.

"And when Captain Maitland offered for me right after Miss Cormier had turned him down, I told him he was after only my fortune, and he was. Everyone knew it, but after I said it, Lady Melbourne told me it was farouche. That I had hurt his feelings."

"We don't like to hear the truth. Some thoughts are better left unsaid, or said only to close friends."

"I didn't say it in public. I said it only to him. Why did he have to tell people what had passed in a private conversation? I had no intention of telling anyone he had offered for me."

"I daresay it was revenge. You called him a name; he wanted to retaliate and called you ill bred. *Entre nous,* I agree with you. It is as well known as an old ballad that Maitland is hanging out for a fortune."

They had reached the end of the hallway and drew to a stop. "I was surprised when your mama wrote inviting me to spend the summer at the castle," Cressida said.

"So was I. I had no notion of it until she told me you had hired the dower house. It seems Lady Brougham mentioned your wanting to get away from society, and as Mama knew she would be missing Tony, she wrote to you." She gave him a considering look. "I did not urge her to do it, if that is what you are asking, but I am very happy she did, and that you are here."

"No, I did not think you could have been

151

behind it when you were so eager to be rid of me."

At the sound of footsteps behind them, they turned. "Brewster, I fear, is hanging out for a dance with you," Dauntry said.

It proved to be the case. Dauntry let her go — reluctantly. She returned to the ballroom and danced with Brewster. When the piano and fiddle struck up a waltz, Dauntry appeared at her side. The ballroom, designed to hold two hundred, was sparsely populated that evening. They had several square yards of space to themselves in which to swoop and sway to the music without bumping into other dancers. It was exhilarating.

"I always thought the waltz should be like this," she said, leaning back in his arms. The chandeliers overhand turned her raven hair to glinting gold. A faraway, dreamy expression swept across her face. She looked like a girl at her first party. His arms tightened. He had to force himself not to kiss her.

When the music was over, she said, "I really should be leaving. Miss Wantage will be wondering what has happened to me. Beau, I fear, will stay until the last dog is hung. He can walk home."

"I shall drive you, and let him take the carriage."

"That is too much trouble, having the

horses put to for such a short drive. Beau can walk home."

"I'll drive you," he repeated, and asked his butler to call his carriage.

"Very well, but you must behave, Dauntry," she said, not in a teasing way, but with perfect sincerity.

If she had said that to a gentleman in London, it would have been repeated abroad, soon taking on the aura of an invitation to dalliance. Dauntry figured that was how she had acquired her racy reputation. "Fear not, I am a tame man in a carriage."

"I doubt that, for you are no tame man on the dance floor. I had no idea dancing with you would be so much fun."

"I have been hiding my light under a mask of gray eminence, as you called it. There was a facer for me! I checked my mirror that night for gray hairs."

"How many did you find?"

"None! I am only five and thirty, after all."

"I am five and twenty, but I would never say 'only' that age. As a general rule, women live longer than men. It is odd that while we are alive, we age so much more quickly, is it not?"

It seemed ludicrous for this young girl to be worried about her age. "You have lost ten years since coming here."

"It is all the seclusion that accounts for it, and the salubrious sea air, of course."

"I hoped your neighbors had something to do with it. And before you tell me how charming Mr. Brewster is, I shall rephrase that utterance. I hoped your landlord had something to do with your amazing rejuvenation."

"Landlady, actually. The house is your mama's. I had best stay clear of her in future, or I shall find myself back in short skirts with my hair down."

"Then we can start all over, as it were, and become childhood sweet — friends."

"I cannot picture you as a child," she said, ignoring that "sweet." "Yet you do look more youthful than before, and less intimidating."

"Intimidating! Good God, you make me sound like an ogre."

"No, only a disapproving judge."

When he took her out to the carriage, Dauntry thought it wiser to sit on the opposite banquette, for he doubted that he would behave himself if he sat beside her. He talked pleasant nonsense for the first while, to show her how far he was from a disapproving judge. As the carriage drove past the road leading to the cottage, Cressida fell silent. He had an idea what she was thinking.

"About Amarylla, Lady deCourcy — or may I call you Cressida? Since I have known you all these years."

"If you like."

"About Amarylla, Cressida —"

"You don't have to explain. I know how bachelors go on. You are not the first man to keep a mistress, and you will not be the last."

"Perhaps I shall not have her here after all."

Dauntry expected her to inquire why he changed his mind, which would have given him an opening to intimate his feelings for her.

She said, "I have changed my mind about the cottage, Dauntry. After being inside, I realize it is too small. The dower house is more suitable. I shall remain there."

Her reply showed clearly she was not thinking along the same lines as himself. She was not feeling this excitement between them. He had read too much into it. "It is a wise decision," he said.

She talked on about her reason for coming to the seaside. "I am considering buying a little cottage on the sea, and wanted to give it a try first, to see how I like it."

"And do you like it?"

"I shall try swimming first and take a trip

on Beau's yacht. If they prove enjoyable, then I might buy a little place. It is too early to tell."

The carriage proceeded to the dower house. When they descended, Dauntry told the driver to take the carriage back. "I shall walk home," he said.

"You might as well have a drive home," she said. "I am afraid I cannot ask you in. Miss Wantage will have retired. I would never hear the end of it if I invited a gentleman in without her there to glower and glare at him and make everyone uncomfortable."

The groom waited, listening with the keenest interest to this exchange until Dauntry waved him off.

"It is a warm evening. I shall enjoy the walk home."

"Well, thank you for a delightful party, Dauntry." She shook his hand. When she tried to remove her fingers, he held on to them.

"I would hardly call it a party," he said, gazing at her face bathed in moonlight.

"It was a wonderful evening, like being home at Tanglewood. A small do, just as I like. I enjoyed the large balls when I first went to London, but after tonight I find I like simple parties even better. You do get to really know — people," she said.

"I hope that means me?"

"Yes, that is what I mean."

"I want to tell you about Amarylla," he said simply.

She placed two fingers on his lips. "Please don't spoil it, Dauntry."

"You are right. Let us end this evening as it should be ended."

Without further speech he pulled her into his arms and kissed her. She was too surprised to be angry at first, and as the kiss deepened, her surprise swelled to astonishment. It was impossible! Dauntry was not French — but he was certainly the same man who had kissed her in the cottage. She couldn't mistake those nibbling kisses that deepened to a bruising attack on her lips, the way his strong fingers splayed on her back, pressing her against him, the heat that flared inside her.

Was she mad? This could not be her mysterious Frenchman. Was she a wanton, to enjoy the kisses of two different men so much? She was too honest to pretend she was not enjoying it. Her arms went around his neck, her fingers reveling in his crisp black hair as she returned every pressure from his lips. Then she forgot the Frenchman, and thought only of Dauntry, who was so very different from what she had expected.

Dauntry, who was bringing his mistress to the cottage . . . There was no explanation for that, only excuses, and she had heard them all from her lady friends. "A gentleman has needs." "It doesn't mean anything to them." How could a kiss like this not mean anything? She drew away and gazed at him with sad, disillusioned eyes.

"Good night, Dauntry," she said in a small voice.

When he reached for her again, she withdrew. "Please don't," she said in a breathless voice. "Once was bad enough."

Then she turned and fled into the house, and Dauntry stood looking at the closed door, wondering if he had heard her aright. "*Bad* enough?" What the devil did she mean by that?

Cressida had a word with Muffet. "Beau may be out until all hours, Muffet. There is no need to wait up for him. He has his key."

"Would you care for a glass of cocoa, missy?"

"Not tonight, thank you. I am tired. I shall go straight up to bed."

This, alas, was impossible. Miss Wantage called her as she tiptoed past the door. "What time is it, dear?" she called.

"Not much past midnight, Miss Wantage. I am sorry if I awoke you."

"I was not asleep. You know I can never sleep until you and Beau are in your beds. Is Beau home?"

"He will be up shortly," Cressida said, wavering between a lie, to let Miss Wantage sleep, and the truth, which would ensure a few more hours of wakefulness.

"Was it a good party?"

"Very nice. Could I get you a glass of warm milk? Muffet it still up."

"I don't like to be a bother to anyone. I'll just glance over a few pages of my Bible to pass the time. What happened to your coiffure, dear? It looks all of a heap."

"The country dance . . ."

"A cap would keep your hair in place. So much neater, and at your age . . ."

"Good night, Miss Wantage."

Cressida escaped to her room, where Jennet had laid out her lawn nightgown and turned down her bed. Miss Wantage was sawing logs in no time; it was Cressida who lay awake, thinking. Dauntry would be spending the weekdays in London. He would be at the seaside only on the weekends, and Amarylla would be at the cottage, so he would be kept busy. She need not see much of him. It would be disastrous to go on seeing him. Society's idea of marriage was not her idea.

She would not go back to London in the autumn. Two Seasons were enough. She would go home, and perhaps marry one of the local gentlemen while she was still young enough to start a nursery.

She heard Beau tiptoe upstairs an hour later. As his room was at the other end of the hall, he did not disturb Miss Wantage's slumber.

Of course, she did not see Dauntry, or have the faintest notion that he had not gone home, but had gone to the cottage, where he spent the better part of an hour searching in vain for the missing letter.

Chapter Eleven

It was close to three o'clock in the morning when Cressida finally slipped into a troubled doze. The quiet clicking of her door handle turning was enough to awaken her. She assumed it was Miss Wantage, with one of her migraines. Cousin Margaret had warned her of them. Dulled by sleep, Cressida sat up, peering into the shadows, as a figure crept silently toward her bed.

"What is it, Miss Wantage?" she asked, trying to dampen the annoyance in her tone.

The shadow stopped. Cressida had raised the blind to allow fresh air into the room. As her eyes became accustomed to the dim light, the shadow began to take on human form. It seemed strange that Miss Wantage did not speak or advance closer to the bed.

"What is it?" Cressida asked with an edge of fear.

Still, there was no reply. The shadow's head turned toward the door. Cressida noticed that the head was smooth and the shoulders broad. Miss Wantage had been wearing her cap with the frilled edge. If she

161

had removed it, her hair would have hung loose. This was not Miss Wantage. It was a man!

"Beau?" she asked sharply. The fear was rising insensibly to panic. "Is that you?"

Instead of answering, the man turned and pelted out of the room. The soft thud of receding footfalls echoed through the open door. Without realizing she was doing it, Cressida opened her lips and emitted a high-pitched scream. She ran to her door, screaming at the top of her lungs.

"Beau! Muffet! Help!"

Within seconds Beau came pelting down the corridor and Miss Wantage's capped head appeared at her door, holding a lighted lamp. This pious dame's first concern was not for the life of her charge, or even her jewelry, but for propriety. She took one look at Beau's pale legs protruding from beneath his nightshirt and covered her eyes.

"Beau! There are ladies present!"

Beau had the sense to ignore her. "Sid, are you all right?"

"A man — in my room."

"Good God!" Miss Wantage said weakly. She did not faint, but she turned white as paper and stood trembling with excitement. "He might have been in my room, too!" she exclaimed. "My room is closer to the stair-

case than yours. I thought I heard something —"

"He went that way," Sid said to Beau,
pointing to the far end of the corridor, where
a curtained archway led to the servants'
stairs.

Beau went darting after him.

"Take a gun, Beau!" Cressida called.

"Put on your robe, Cressida," Miss Wantage said.

Cressida ran into her room and picked up
the poker, as Beau had not heeded her warning to get a gun.

"Your robe!" Miss Wantage called after
her as she ran, wearing nothing but her
nightgown, toward the stairs after Beau.
"What will the intruder think of you . . ."
Her voice petered out.

As Cressida ran carefully down the narrow, unlit servants' stairs, she heard a scuffle
in the kitchen. It sounded as if Beau had
cornered the intruder. Turning the bend in
the stairs, she could hear the men gasping
and thrashing about on the floor. There was
not enough light to be certain which one she
would hit if she used the poker, and she did
not know where the lamps in the kitchen
were located, so she stood at the ready. If
the intruder won, she would whack him on
the side of the head when he stood up.

One man rolled aside and scrambled to his feet. "Beau?" she called, and was answered by a grunt from the floor.

When she turned back to the other man, he was already heading for the back door. He overturned the kitchen maid's stool behind him. It caught Cressida a sharp blow on the shin, temporarily disabling her. It was long enough for the man to unlock the kitchen door and flee into the night. He took one look over his shoulder before he darted off. Cressida fully expected to see the face of the man who called himself Melbury. In the pale rays of moonlight she saw a black mask, which made the whole affair even more frightening.

She bolted the door, lit a lamp, and went to Beau's assistance. "Are you all right?"

He rose, gasping for breath and rubbing the back of his head. "He was a strong lout. He caught my head between his two hands and banged it on the floor."

"Good gracious! He might have broken your skull."

"He might have killed me — but I had the feeling he didn't really want to hurt me. It wasn't a very hard bang, and he was strong."

"How very civil of him!" Cressida sneered.

The racket was enough to bring Mrs. Armstrong forth from her bedroom, which was just off the kitchen for convenience's sake. She appeared with her white hair hanging in a tail down her back. True to England, her sleeping attire continued her color theme with a white gown, blue robe, and a red ribbon tying her braided tail.

"What is all the ruckus?" she demanded. "Why are you dashing about in the middle of the night, next-door to naked?"

Although less squeamish than Miss Wantage, she was no lecher and went into her bedroom to provide the youngsters with something to cover their sins. She handed Beau a patchwork quilt and Cressida her own Sunday-best shawl.

While Cressida and Beau recounted their adventure, she stoked up the smoldering fire and put on a kettle.

When she had heard the gist of it, she said, "Why don't the pair of you go up to the saloon and be comfortable? I'll bring you up a nice cup of tea as soon as it's brewed. No need to rouse up Old Muffet. Age wants ease. Let him rest."

As the seating in the kitchen was rudimentary, they did as she suggested.

"Who do you think it was?" Beau asked when they were settled in above stairs.

"It cannot have been Melbury. He is supposed to be in Bath. The man was the size and shape of the brash swaggerer who called, pretending he was Brewster. His covering his face suggests we would recognize him. Of more interest, Beau, what was he after? He was not carrying off the silver."

"No, and not locking for it upstairs either, I shouldn't think."

"He might have been after my jewelry," she said.

"Or you," Beau added with a warning look.

She drew Tory's shawl more closely about her. "Don't say such things. You're making my flesh crawl. How did he get in? Are you sure you locked the door after you when you came home?"

"Positive."

They went to check and found the front door locked and bolted. The kitchen door had also been locked. The French doors in the library were the only other doors to the outside. When they checked, the doors were ajar, but there was no sign of a forced entry.

"Is it possible he has a key?" Cressida asked, worried for the future. "Muffet would certainly have locked this door when he made his rounds. I don't believe it has ever been open since we came here."

When Tory brought the tea, they asked her about it.

"I feared as much. I have been thinking about it, and I've figured out how it happened," she said. "I left the library door on the latch when I went out this evening — just to have a word with Cook at the castle, since you were both away. I enjoy the bit of fresh air. I have no key to the front door, you see, and I saw no point in bothering Old Muffet."

"Why did you not lock the library doors when you came home?" Cressida asked. She knew from Tory's averted eyes that she was making this tale up out of whole cloth.

"That's his job, isn't it? He don't like interfering with his chores. No doubt he thought I had locked it. Another time, I'll make sure one of us tends to it."

"Do you not have a key to the back door?" Beau asked.

"I do, but when I got home, I found out I'd forgotten to take it with me."

"Why did you leave the library doors on the latch if you thought you had the back door key with you?" he persisted.

Without a blink of delay Tory had her lie ready. "It's the rats," she said. "Jennet spotted a rat hiding under the back stoop. If there were rats about, I meant to use the library

167

doors. It's not pleasant to have a rat run up your leg. Then, when I discovered I'd left my keys behind, I went and used the library doors. I'll have the rat catcher in tomorrow to be rid of the vermin."

"Would you have any idea who the intruder might be?" Cressida asked. She knew she would not hear the truth, but by the process of elimination, she might discover who it was not, at least.

"Very likely it was young Melbury again."

"He is in Bath."

Tory gave her a sharp lock. "No, he isn't," she said, surprised. She looked Cressida right in the eye as she spoke. So she was telling the truth then. "I didn't want to distress you, milady, but he was seen hereabouts this very day."

Beau and Cressida exchanged a questioning look. "Supposing it was Melbury," Beau said, "what do you think he was after upstairs? Is it possible he meant to — harm Lady deCourcy?"

"Attack her in her bed, do you mean?" she asked, astounded at such a charge. "Not he! He can have his pick of the common village women. Why would he risk putting his neck in a noose by attacking a lady? Sure Melbury never had to use force in that way. He is all honey and sweet talk. The Dauntrys have taken a good deal from him, but they would draw the line at that, I promise you."

"He was not looking for teaspoons in my bedroom, Tory," Cressida said reasonably.

"No, that was not the silver he was after. His aunt Annie used to have a silver dresser set there of a comb and brush and mirror and I don't know what all. We moved it when we learned you were coming. She left it to him in her will, but he never bothered to pick it up, for he said if he took it he'd only hawk it, and he wanted it for a keepsake of his auntie. A heirloom, as they say. Likely he is in dun territory and dropped by to pick it up tonight."

"In the middle of the night, wearing a mask?" Beau added with a disbelieving eye.

"If he is supposed to be in Bath, then he wouldn't want to be recognized in case the Dauntrys learned he is here. I believe his lordship had a bit of a falling-out with his cousin and sent him to Bath for a spell."

It was clear they were to get no more information out of this accomplished liar. She was dismissed, and Cressida and Beau just sighed.

"We'll never know," Beau said. "That woman can lie faster than a dog shakes his tail. She ought to be in Parliament."

"I think she was telling the truth about

Melbury being in the neighborhood. We caught her off guard, and she accidentally blurted out the truth."

"But she was lying about the dresser set and about our intruder being Melbury," Beau said. "She wore her shifty look when she said it."

"Odd she would put the blame on him, as he is such a favorite. She tried to dilute his guilt by that story about the heirloom. She must be protecting someone she likes even better than Melbury. Who could it be?"

"Dauntry?" Beau suggested. "The size was about right."

"No, he is a little taller. He would not come into my bedchamber, Beau. If there were anything here he wanted, he could have got it before we came. I cannot believe he was after my jewelry. No, I don't believe it was Dauntry at all."

"If it wasn't Dauntry, and it wasn't Melbury, then who was it? Allan Brewster?"

Neither of them believed this unexceptionable gentleman had suddenly turned into a ken smasher.

"It must have been a tramp," Cressida said.

"A tramp who knew his way about the house very well," Beau said disbelievingly.

"Well, a local tramp," she said.

They left it at that, although they both felt in their bones this was not the answer.

Miss Wantage still had to be informed of the story and pacified before they could retire for what remained of the night. She insisted on having Jennet hauled from her bed. A truckle bed was brought from the servants' quarters for Jennet, who spent the hours until daylight inside Miss Wantage's locked door in case the villain came back. It was either that, or Miss Wantage would bunk in with Cressida, who was in no mood to accommodate her after such a harrowing night.

Of course, her precautions were unnecessary. Their caller did not return. As Beau said to Cressida just before yawning his way off to his room, "Pity he hadn't gone into her room. One look at Wantage and the fellow would not show his nose around here again. The fact of the matter is, she is jealous as a green cow that you were the one he chose." None of which was much consolation to Cressida.

One other suspect occurred to her as she lay in bed, staring at the door. The desk she had pushed in front of it to ward off interlopers formed a dark rectangle against the white square of door. The intruder could have been the Frenchman who was talking to Dauntry at the cottage. Thus far, she had not revealed to Dauntry that she had seen him there the night of her attack. She sat straight up in bed as another idea occurred to her. He might have been looking for it, the mysterious *elle* they had spoken of! It was time to reveal all, and demand that Dauntry do the same.

Chapter Twelve

After such a restless night, Cressida slept until nine the next morning. Sunlight streamed in at the window, gilding the rich mahogany of the furnishings and making a mockery of the desk barring the door. It seemed impossible that a strange man had found his way into this civilized sanctuary the night before. She had learned that sunlight, on the coast, did not necessarily mean a warm day. Much depended on the direction and force of the wind. The swaying treetops told her the wind was from the sea, and thus cool. She wore a serge suit, for she meant to go out that morning to do some investigating regarding the intruder.

First she would call at the castle and tell Dauntry of the break-in. She was also curious to spy on the cottage to see if it was being prepared for the arrival of Amarylla. "Perhaps I shall not have her here," Dauntry had said, which was not the same as saying "I shall not have her." A trip to Beachy Head was on the agenda as well, to see if there were any strange men in the village. When she went into the hallway, she saw Miss Wantage speaking to a man at the door of her room. The man wore a fustian jacket and spoke in colloquial accents.

Miss Wantage spotted Cressida and said, "I do not know what precautions you plan to take to prevent further assaults, my dear, but I had Muffet send off at first light for the locksmith to install a new lock on my door, and I suggest that you do the same. I have just been discussing the matter of the windows with Crump."

Crump lifted an imaginary hat and ducked his head in the direction of Lady deCourcy.

"Short of installing bars, Crump sees no way of ensuring our safety, for as he so rightly points out, any child can smash a pane of glass and climb in," Miss Wantage continued.

"That is out of the question, Miss Wantage," Cressida said. "The house does not belong to me. Quite apart from the expense, I cannot turn Lady Dauntry's house into a fortress."

"She can hardly refuse permission, when we have been assaulted in our beds."

"We were not assaulted in our beds!" Cressida exclaimed. What was the woman thinking of, to send such wicked gossip through the village? Crump was listening with his ears stretched. "He was not in your room at all."

"He most certainly was! I told you last night I had heard something. A low, fiendish laugh. This morning I found dirt on the carpet, from his feet."

"From the truckle bed you had brought down from the attic, more likely. Really, Miss Wantage, all this is not necessary. There is no point even asking to have the windows barred. Dauntry would think we had ran mad."

Miss Wantage drew her ears back like an angry mare. "Some ladies might enjoy being assaulted by strange men. For myself, if you cannot ensure my safety, I am very much afraid I shall have to return to Bath."

"I should be very sorry to lose you. I hope you will reconsider," Cressida said, and left before she said what she really thought. Hurray! Go — go back to Bath, go to Timbuktu for all I care.

She was surprised to find Beau still at the table, gazing out the window and holding a cup of coffee.

"You slept in as well, I see," she said, taking up a plate to help herself from the sideboard.

"I have been up since seven. Nick says the wind is too high to take the *Sea Dog* out, but

175

he thinks it is lessening, and we can go out this afternoon."

Cressida sat down and attacked her gammon and eggs. She told him of Miss Wantage's latest folly. "She threatens to leave!"

"Shall I run over to Beachy Head and hire a band, to celebrate?"

"It would be no tragedy, but I would have to find someone to replace her. Perhaps Lady Dauntry can suggest some local lady."

"Save your breath. You could not drive Wantage off with a herd of wild horses. She sticks like a burr. Oh, by the bye, I was over at the cottage."

"Is there anything afoot there?" Cressida asked.

"Dauntry's lightskirt has arrived. I got a peek at her at the upstairs window."

Cressida's shoulders stiffened. She jabbed a fork angrily into a piece of gammon to release her temper. "I see. Was Dauntry there to welcome her?"

"There was no one else that I could see. No movement downstairs, but of course, I only watched from outside."

"Perhaps he was in the bedchamber with her."

"Very likely. She's dashed pretty. I always liked those blondes."

Cressida tossed her raven curls. "Yes, they

176

seem to be in vogue this year." Then she frowned. "Blond, did you say?"

"Yes, she had her hair out loose. She looked like a princess from a fairy tale."

"But Amarylla is a brunette! She is supposed to be his *chère amie.*"

"Really? Then he must be importing a harem, for the stunner I saw was a blonde, and no mistake about it. She was brushing out her hair. She leapt away from the window when she saw me, as if she were trying to hide. Odd way for a lightskirt to behave. They ain't usually shy of flaunting their charms."

Cressida soon made sense of it. He did not want her to see his bit of muslin. "Dauntry had ordered her to lie low, I expect. He passes for a man of character."

"Then why bring her here? There are no secrets in a place like this. I am going up to the castle now to inform Dauntry of our break-in. I was just waiting a bit to see if you would care to go with me."

Cressida was so furious, she would not have asked Dauntry for help if the house had been burning down around her. "You go ahead, Beau. Very likely he is not home. Try the cottage."

"If he ain't home, I'll leave word for him to call. Not the thing to go knocking on his

177

door when he is with his woman. He would think me a regular Johnny Flat. I'm off, then, if you think you're safe here without me."

"The man won't come back in broad daylight."

"I was speaking of Wantage," he said, and left.

Cressida pushed her breakfast aside. She was just sipping at her coffee when Muffet showed Dauntry into the morning parlor.

Icicles hung on her curt greeting. "Good morning, Lord Dauntry." He bowed and returned the greeting. She decided to behave as though she cared nothing for his lechery. "Would you like a cup of coffee?"

"Thank you," he said, taking up a chair across the table. "I hope it is hot. There seems to be a chill in the air this morning." He directed a questioning look at her.

"Yes," she replied, pretending to misunderstand him. "Beau mentioned the wind is high." She poured the coffee and handed it to him. "You got here very quickly. Beau must have met you on his way to the castle."

"Beau? I have not seen him. I was at the cottage."

"I see," she said in a thin voice.

He assumed her anger was at his not allowing her to move into the cottage. "Someone has been there," he said.

"Has been?" she asked, startled. "Do you mean she has left already?"

"She? Why do you assume it was a woman?"

"Beau saw her."

"Did he, by God! What did she look like?"

"Blond. Like a princess from a fairy tale. He did not really get much of a look at her. Beau was just passing by this morning. Are you saying you don't know who the woman is?"

"I haven't the least notion."

"One of Amarylla's friends, perhaps?" she suggested with a sapient look.

"Amarylla will not be coming," he said, lowering his brow. "I tried to tell you last night. The reason I am here is to see if you had any trouble from the person who had broken into the cottage. The door had been forced open."

"If you can call sneaking right into my bedchamber in the middle of the night trouble, then I suppose I had, but it was no blond lady. It was a man."

Dauntry's cup hit the saucer with considerable force. He stared at her in disbelief. "What? A man right in your bedchamber? Are you all right?"

She basked in pleasure to see his consternation. "I seem to have survived," she said, looking down to ensure that she was all there and in good shape. "In future, however, I do wish you would tell your French friend that in England it is the custom to knock on a lady's door before barging in."

Dauntry lifted his cup and took a slow sip of coffee. He set the cup down, gazing at Cressida all the while. "So you were awake that night. I had hoped —"

"Hoped that you had put me hors de combat with that blanket? Sorry to disoblige you, but I overheard it all."

"You have good ears." His lips stretched in a teasing smile. "And very soft lips, mam'selle. Or so my — er, French friend tells me. It was he who wrapped you in the blanket, by the bye."

Cressida studied his expression, trying to gauge his meaning. Which one of them had kissed her? Dauntry was enjoying this charade. She decided to play along. "You may tell your French friend that he also has delightful lips. But he still should knock before entering — and he should also ask permission before taking advantage of a lady."

"I shall inform him you approve of his lechery but object to his lack of manners. As to the break-in here, however, it was not my French friend. He was at my own house last night. Knowing his French way with the ladies, I felt he and you — were safer with him there."

After a pausing frown, she replied, "But if the intruder was not your French friend, and he was not Melbury— Actually, Tory says Melbury is in the neighborhood."

"Tory lies."

"I know, but I think she was telling the truth about Melbury. I don't suppose his aunt Annie left him a silver dresser set, which he left here for safekeeping?"

"She left him a few trinkets, all of which he promptly sold. Melbury is a young fool, but he would not risk my displeasure by invading a house Mama had leased to a noble lady. He prefers to keep his crimes within the family and close circle of friends, who are not likely to have him locked up, you see. I have known him forever. He is crooked as a dog's hind leg, but he don't prey on strangers. Not in that fashion, at least. He might charm a trinket out of a lady, but he would not steal it. Your caller was not Melbury."

"Then who was he?"

"Are you quite certain there was a man there? I had a spinster aunt who used to imagine something of the sort."

Her nostrils pinched dangerously. "I do not imagine men in my room. Beau did not imagine the bump on his head. Nor did Miss

Wantage imagine that she heard him in her room. Well, actually, I think she did imagine it. I do not for one moment believe that fiendish laugh, but Beau did not imagine having his head banged on the floor. And you must tell her she cannot put bars on her window, Dauntry. It is really the outside of enough."

Dauntry cupped his chin in his hand and studied her. She looked remarkably like an angry kitten. "Are you sure it was Beau whose head was knocked on the floor?"

"Miss Wantage has the local locksmith in her bedroom this very minute."

"Shame on her — and you. I am shocked that you permit such carrying-on, milady. If Wantage is feeling lonesome, she might at least hang out for a gentleman."

"Oh, you are too provoking! It is not funny."

"I do not take the matter lightly, Cressida," he said, gazing at her with the residue of a smile. "I shall speak to the local constable and personally take every precaution — short of installing bars on the windows — to ensure your safety. A couple of footmen will patrol the house tonight, for starters."

"But what does the man want? Is it the letter?"

At her words, Dauntry's face froze into a

perfect mask of innocence. "Letter? What letter is that?" he asked in a wooden voice.

"The one you were looking for at the cottage, of course. Why should he think it is here, when it was, presumably, supposed to be at the cottage?"

Dauntry rose and drew a chair closer to hers. "As you know nine-tenths of the story, I might as well tell you the rest. You will have observed that my cove here offers the best landing facilities for a ship."

"Dauntry, pray do not tell me you are a common smuggler!"

"Ships from France bring things other than brandy and silk. Sometimes they bring certain messages — *vous comprenez?*"

"Letters regarding the doings of Boney's army?"

"More or less. Those letters are left at the cottage. I cannot always be there in person to receive them. If the revenuemen caught me consorting with smugglers, it would look bad for all Whigs. It is because of the letters that I could not let you have the cottage."

"You might have had them left at the dower house," she said, adopting a moue.

"I might, but we let various relatives use this place in the summer. If you were not here, then Cousin Jerome and his family, or Aunt Lydia, or someone would expect to use it. The cottage was safer. There was a shipment of brandy landed earlier this week. I was eagerly awaiting the letter that was to come with it. An associate tells me the letter was delivered to the cottage, but it was not found in its customary place. I have scoured the house from top to bottom without finding it."

"You think someone took it, someone who might use it against us?"

"That is one possibility, although the letters are always in code. No, my major concern is that someone who has no notion of its importance has picked it up. I want to find the letter. The Foreign Office is most eager to get it."

"I see. But it was not you who sent a man here last night to search for it?"

"Certainly not. I have no reason to think it is here. My information is that it was left at the cottage. One of the English fellows who lands the cargo gets the letters from one of the French sailors. My man took it to the cottage, as usual."

"Where does he leave it in the cottage?"

"Inside the Bible that is always in the parlor. The Bible is there, in its usual place. The letter is not."

"You think the blond woman was looking for it?"

"I don't see how she could be aware of its existence. My go-between is marble constant. He has two sons in Wellington's army. No, I think the woman is just an itinerant who saw an empty house and sought a night's free lodging."

"Well, I am very sorry about your letter, Dauntry. It seems it cannot be connected with my intruder after all."

"I can do nothing more about the letter except keep looking. Your intruder is another matter. For the meanwhile, it might be best if you and your party remove to the castle."

Cressida considered the offer but finally declined it. "Thank you, but we have been enough trouble already. With a couple of footmen to keep guard, we shall be safe here. Beau felt the man was not really vicious. He did not bang his head as hard on the floor as he might have."

Dauntry stared. "Very civil of him, I'm sure. More important, did he touch you?"

"No, my charms proved no temptation at all. It was very dark," she added when his lips moved uncertainly. "He ran like a rabbit when I screamed. He seemed to know his way about the house. It was pitch-black in the corridor, but he ran straight for the backstairs and out the kitchen door."

"Some local fellow, seeing what he could pick up. Someone who served here as footman or groom in the past, likely, and did not realize the house had been let."

"It is odd a local would not know it. Any doings at the castle must be discussed in the neighborhood. We have been to Beachy Head, too."

"That is true. Yet a passing ken smasher would not know his way about the house. In fact, very few people would."

"Melbury would," she said.

Dauntry shook his head. "No, I do not believe it was Melbury."

"The intruder was the size of the fellow who came here calling himself Brewster."

"I'll have a word with Brewster."

"Why not have a word with Tory? She would know if the man was Melbury. The man who first called, I mean."

"A good point."

Cressida rang for her. She came to the door, looking as if she were confronting a pair of lions. "What can I do for you, milady?" she asked.

"You can tell us who Lady deCourcy's mysterious caller was, Tory," Dauntry said. "The one you pretended was Melbury."

"It was Melbury, milord," she said with a guilty look.

"You know perfectly well he is in Bath."

"Well, he looked like Melbury. They do say we all have a double of ourselves on the earth," she added lamely.

Dauntry turned to Cressida in disgust. "This is pointless. I'll speak to Brewster. He might have some idea who it could be."

Tory turned tail and fled from the room.

"Can't you make her tell you?" Cressida said.

"She is protecting someone. She wouldn't tell if you yanked every tooth from her head one by one."

Cressida winced at this brutal speech. "Who would she lie to protect?"

"Any of my family. She is faithful to a fault. She means no harm, you know. You can at least console yourself that your caller had no evil intentions, or Tory would be the first one after him with a poker. And now, most reluctantly, I shall leave you."

He seized her hand and raised it to his lips. Cressida felt a warm weakness invade her.

"What were you trying to tell me about Amarylla, Dauntry?" she asked in a breathless voice.

He lifted his eyes and gave a wicked smile. "I had toyed with the notion of moving her into the cottage to keep you away. And to make you jealous," he added.

"I see. And are you no longer eager to make me jealous?"

"Surely we have gone beyond that stage, you and I."

"Speak for yourself. I was jealous as a green cow when Beau thought you had opened up a harem at the cottage."

Dauntry paused over that statement. "I hardly know whether to be flattered, or find Beau and give his head another tap on the floor. Harem indeed!" She smiled indulgently. "Does he think I am made of gold? It would cost a fortune."

"Dauntry!"

"I can scarcely handle one lady, let alone a whole harem. I shall be back this afternoon. Don't let any more strange men into your boudoir."

They were interrupted by a bustle at the doorway as Miss Wantage came in. "Thank God you have come!" she exclaimed, rushing up to Dauntry. "I see Cressida has been telling you about the assault. What are you going to do about it? A lock on the door is useless when anyone with a club can break down the windows and ravage us."

Cressida said, "Dauntry is sending down two footmen, Miss Wantage, and speaking to the constable."

"The constable," she said with a dismissing sniff. "If he is anything like the men in Bath, it is a waste of time. Some villain stole the door knocker right off Cousin Margaret's door in broad daylight. I gave the constable a perfect description of him, for I caught a glimpse of him as he hightailed it around the corner. A man in a fustian coat with a face like a thief — and they refused to find him. Two footmen, you say? Surely we require at least three. There are three doors."

"Three footmen," Dauntry agreed.

"What about all the windows?"

"The footmen would hear if the glass was broken," he said, reining in his temper.

"You may be sure they will be sawing logs within an hour of their posting."

"What do you suggest, Miss Wantage?" Dauntry asked.

When she looked at his forbidding expression, she hadn't the fortitude to suggest bars on the windows.

"A dog," Dauntry said for her. "I shall send down an insomniac hound, fed with strong coffee, to guard the house."

Miss Wantage considered this and found it satisfactory. "There now," she said triumphantly to Cressida. "I told you Lord Dauntry would handle it, when you said it was pointless to ask him."

Dauntry turned a kindling eye on Cressida, who stood with her mouth open in astonishment.

"We'll catch the bounder tonight when he comes back after me," Miss Wantage continued. "I must go and ask Muffet to pay Crump before he leaves. You can settle up with Muffet later, Cressida."

She sailed out of the saloon, actually wearing a smile.

Dauntry just shook his head. "I shall return, Saint Cressida. I want to thank you from the bottom of my heart for not accepting my injudicious offer to remove your household to the castle. And by the bye, what was that remark she let slip about it being pointless to ask Dauntry for help?"

"Pray do not harass me, Dauntry. One impossible friend at a time is enough."

"At least you call me friend. That will have to do — for now. Though how you can find it in your heart to call that shrew one is beyond me."

He looked to the doorway to see they were alone, stole a quick kiss, and left.

Chapter Thirteen

Cressida's spirits were much improved after Dauntry's visit. She was still concerned about the man who had broken into the house, and about the missing letter, but her romance with Dauntry was a great consolation. Was it possible she had finally found a man she could love, and who could love her, with all her faults? She went out to ask Muffet if Beau had returned. He had not, which suggested he had gone for a ride without her.

"By the bye," she asked, "how much do I owe you for Miss Wantage's lock?"

When he told her the price, she said, "That is rather dear. I hope it is a good, stout lock."

"That is for both locks," Muffet replied.

"Both of them? Oh, she had one put on my door as well, though I told her not to."

"I believe 'twas Mrs. Armstrong who asked for the other lock, missy."

"I see."

Mrs. Armstrong ought to have spoken to her first, but Cressida was not a hard mistress. She thought no more of it, but went to change into her riding habit. Beau would likely return soon, and they could ride out together. As she passed the attic door en route to her chamber, she noticed a shiny new padlock on the door. Miss Wantage came poking her head out to see why Cressida had come upstairs. One of the lady's most annoying features was her rampant curiosity.

"Why did Tory have the attic padlocked?" Cressida asked.

"Why, I assumed you had asked her to do so, my dear. You never mean she took it upon herself to do it without speaking to you? Encroaching creature! Mind you, I thought it an excellent idea, considering the wailing that went on up there the night we arrived. Who is to say the villain has not been up there all along?"

"Did Tory give you the key?"

"No, I made sure she would give it to Muffet."

"Muffet said nothing to me."

Cressida returned below stairs at once and summoned Mrs. Armstrong.

"I would like to know why you had a new lock installed on the attic door without consulting me, Tory," she said.

"Why, for your own protection, milady, to

be sure. Miss Wantage seemed mighty taken with the idea."

"I am the mistress of this household," she reminded her headstrong housekeeper. "If you will just give me the key." She held out her hand in a peremptory manner.

"You'll never believe what that Crump went and did, milady. I blame myself entirely, for I ought to have checked before he left. Didn't the gudgeon walk off and leave the wrong set of keys with me. They don't open the door."

"Mrs. Armstrong, give me the keys at once, or I shall take an ax and batter the door down."

"They don't work," Tory said, and took out two keys held together on a tin ring. She began to remove one key.

"I'll take them both," Cressida said.

Tory handed over the two keys. Cressida marched up to the attic while Tory tagged along, offering excuses and explanations.

Cressida ignored her. She inserted one of the keys in the lock. It turned smoothly with a quiet click.

"Well now," Tory said in simulated astonishment. "The oil I asked the backhouse boy to put in the lock has done a world of good. Did you ever see the likes? It must have been rusted."

As Cressida flung the attic door open, Tory hastily leapt to the stairs in front of her and began speaking in a loud tone, pitching her voice up the staircase.

"You will not find anything you shouldn't, milady. There is nothing up here but bat droppings and lumber."

She reached the landing two seconds before her mistress and looked all about, drew an audible sigh of relief, and smiled at Cressida. "There, you see, it is just as I said. Not a soul up here."

As she spoke, she attempted to hustle Cressida back down. Cressida pushed her aside and marched into the second room. She saw the mattress on the floor by the window, the roll of blankets, the pitcher of lemonade, and the plate of biscuits. E'er long, she espied the tip of a head protruding above a dresser.

"Come out of there at once," Cressida said in her most imperious tone, expecting to see the man who called himself Brewster.

The head rose a few inches higher, revealing a tousle of blond curls, a pair of wide-set blue eyes, and a dainty, retroussé nose.

"Good God! It's a woman!" Cressida exclaimed.

The young woman sidled out from behind the dresser. Her traveling suit was wrinkled and spotted with stains, but it was an exceedingly fashionable suit of blue worsted.

"You must be Lady deCourcy," a shy voice said. The woman — girl, really — curtsied.

"Who the devil are you?" Cressida asked.

"I'm Tony," the girl said, and burst into tears.

"Why, as I live and breathe. If it isn't Lady Antonia, from the castle!" Tory explained with a wary look.

Cressida stood openmouthed until she had grasped the situation. "But, my dear, you are supposed to be on your honeymoon at the Lake District. What are you doing here, cowering in a musty old attic?"

The tears deepened to sobs that so befogged the girl's explanation, there was no making heads nor tails of it.

"She left him," Tory said.

When Cressida conquered her astonishment, she said in a gentle voice, "Come downstairs, my dear. There is no need to hide from me."

The single word "Dauntry" emerged from a garbled jumble of sounds.

Cressida spoke to Tory. "I am taking Lady Antonia downstairs. Pray bring hot bathwater to the Rose Suite, and a change of clothes. If Lady Antonia has no clothes with her, bring some of mine. They will be too large, but at least they are clean." The Rose Suite was chosen as being the farthest removed from Miss Wantage.

"I'll send Jennet to lend her a hand. Her ladyship is a mite shy of strangers," Tory said, and went below stairs to draw the bathwater.

The sobbing girl turned a grateful eye on her hostess. "Please don't tell Dauntry," she said as Cressida opened the door to leave.

In Cressida's opinion, Dauntry certainly had to be told, but she did not wish to alarm the shy creature further.

"We shall have a good cose after you have made a toilette," she said.

"Thank you, ma'am. You are not nearly so bad as Tory said."

Cressida went downstairs, where there was a great rushing about of servants bringing water and fresh linen and conferring on this new development. It turned out Lady Harold, for such was now her legal name, had brought one gown with her, which Tory took away to press. While this was going forth, Cressida went to the saloon to collect her wits. It was obviously Lady Harold whom Tory had been harboring in the attic when first they arrived. When Tory realized her new mistress was curious, she had bundled the girl off to the cottage, which accounted for the silver tray and good china being at the back door. She was the blond lady Beau had seen at the window. After she had been spotted there, she had come running back to the dower house. Tory had ordered new keys to keep her mistress out of the attics. Many mysteries were now explained, but a new one was still to be uncovered. Why had Antonia left an unexceptionable husband on her honeymoon? Cressida could not believe Dauntry had handed his young sister over to a villain. It was some foolish lovers' quarrel.

It was close to an hour later when Tory appeared at the door of the saloon, leading a refreshed Lady Harold behind her. With her golden curls brushed, her face washed, and wearing a pretty green sprigged muslin gown, she looked attractive in spite of her pallor and unhappiness.

"There you go, now, missy," Tory said, pushing the girl forward. "Her ladyship's bark is a deal worse than her bite. Just tell her your story and I make no doubt she will know what is best to do. She knows everything," she added with a gimlet shot from her blue eyes.

"Bring us tea, Tory," Cressida said.

"I will, but what you'd ought to do is get

a glass of wine into her, for the poor soul is trembling like a leaf."

Tory left, and Lady Harold entered the room uncertainly, staring at Cressida like a frightened doe confronting a hunter.

"I am very sorry for the trouble I have caused you, ma'am."

Cressida showed her to a seat and followed Tory's advice. The girl needed wine to put her at her ease.

"It was no trouble, Lady Harold." The girl winced at the name. "Indeed, there was no reason to hide from me. I should be happy to help you in any way I can."

"No one can help me. I am ruined," the girl said, fresh tears starting in her eyes.

"I collect you are referring to your marriage?"

"To our wedding night, Lady deCourcy!"

"Ah." This was unfamiliar ground to Cressida, but she had heard from friends that it was not always the bed of roses they had anticipated. "I believe that sort of thing becomes easier with time," she said vaguely.

"Oh, it is not that! Harold ran away. He went downstairs immediately after dinner to blow a cloud and never came back."

"You mean he disappeared? But that is dreadful. You ought to have called a constable."

"The innkeeper did call one. They took Harold away to the roundhouse. He was drunk as a Dane — on our wedding night!" She stopped to bawl for a moment, then continued. "He drank a deal of wine at dinner, but he must have drunk more downstairs. I waited for hours, and when I heard the ruckus below, I went to peek over the banister, and saw him — drunk. He hates me. It is clear now that his mama forced him into this marriage. I had nowhere to go, so I came home. I filled my bandbox and took the bit of money I could find in the room and caught the stage home. Luckily we had gotten only as far as Tunbridge Wells. I got off before the coach entered Beachy Head so no one would see me and tell Dauntry and Mama. I had to walk all the way home, only, of course, I could not go home, so I came here, because I knew Tory was here. I am very sorry if I inconvenienced you, ma'am."

"You were also at the cottage?"

"Yes, Tory said I would have to leave, or you would find me and tell Dauntry. He arranged the match, you see, and would ring a peal over me for making such a botch of it."

Cressida gave a start of alarm. "When you say he arranged the match, do you mean you were not in favor of it?"

"Oh, no! I was very fond of Harold then, before I knew what he was like. Dauntry arranged the dowry and all that sort of thing. Oh, whatever am I to do, Lady deCourcy?"

The tea tray arrived, carried in by Muffet, who behaved with perfect discretion, just faintly smiling at the young lady to make her welcome. Antonia appeared to be in good appetite. She stirred six teaspoons of sugar and half the pitcher of milk into her tea, and took a handful of macaroons. While Cressida served tea, her mind was busy considering what ought to be done.

At length she said, "What you have to decide is whether you wish to give it a try with Lord Harold, or have the marriage annulled."

"I gave it a try with Harold. He was so disgusted, he went below stairs and drank himself into a quarrel."

Cressida, having no firsthand knowledge of Lord Harold, hardly knew what to say. "If you are determined that the marriage would not work, then I think you must tell Dauntry, and let him make the arrangements to end it."

Antonia's sulks and moues said clearly that this was not what she wanted. "Dauntry will be very angry," she said. "He told me I was too young."

"It is possible, of course, that Lord Harold was just nervous about the wedding night. He might have gone below to have a glass for courage, and got carried away."

"But why has he not come after me again? He came looking for me only the once. You know, the time he said he was Allan Brewster." A smile peeped out, causing two dimples at the corners of her lips. "I wish I could have seen it. Tory said he was as nervous as a tick, talking loud and trying to behave like Melbury to fool you, only he overdid it. Harold is not like that at all. He is really quite shy."

"That was Lord Harold! But why did Tory not arrange for you to meet him?"

"I told her to tell him I was not here if he came. I meant it only to frighten him a little. I made sure he would come back. He *must* know where I am. Where else could I be? He knows I could not go to the castle because of Dauntry."

"I believe he has been back," Cressida said, and gave Lady Harold a slightly abridged version of the caller who had frightened them all out of their wits the night before. She omitted that he had gone into her bedroom. Antonia seemed the foolish sort of girl who would pretend to think he had done it on purpose.

"I was in the cottage last night," she said. "Tory sent Jennet over to bear me company, for I could not like to be alone in the house at smugglers' cove. It was very boring, being there alone for hours, and sometimes I had to run to the attic to hide, for Dauntry kept coming to the cottage. So contrary of him. He hardly ever goes there."

They were interrupted by a sharp rap from the door knocker.

"Harold!" Antonia squealed, jumping up.

"More likely Dauntry," Cressida warned.

"Oh, he must not see me!"

Antonia darted from the room. Within seconds Lord Dauntry was shown in. He took one look at Cressida's face and said, "I am not armed, I promise you. It is purely a social call."

He looked at the tea tray and said, "Good. I am just in time for tea."

"I hope you will join me," she said, glancing nervously at Antonia's cup and the nibbled macaroons on her plate.

Chapter Fourteen

"I see you have already had company," Dauntry said, glancing at the second teacup on the table. "If it had not been a lady, I should be jealous, Cressida."

"Why do you assume it was a lady?" she asked.

"Because I saw the tail of a skirt disappear around the corner as I came in. Who was your caller? I hope I did not frighten her away."

"I had no caller. It — it was Jennet," she said, and felt her cheeks burning. She had not Mrs. Armstrong's talent for prevarication. She should have said Miss Wantage!

"Has Jennet taken to wearing sprigged muslin in lieu of an apron?"

"The gown was mine. She was trying it on for me. It requires shortening. We are about the same height."

"And taking tea with you while she was about it?"

"It seemed uncivil not to offer her a cup. I took your hint about generosity to the servants."

"I had no idea you paid me so much heed — nor misunderstood me so entirely. There is a difference between generosity and equality. Pray do not consider it necessary to invite Jennet to join you for dinner."

"If you say so, Dauntry. Naturally, your wish is my command."

His eyebrows rose. "Hmmm. That suggests interesting possibilities," he murmured.

"Don't get your hopes up. We are speaking only of my treatment of your servants."

"I knew there would be a catch in it," he said, brushing an imaginary fleck of dust from his sleeve. "Mama thinks you should remove to the castle until the intruder is found. I think so, too. You are acquiring bad habits from your housekeeper. That was an interesting series of lies you have tried to palm off on me, Cressida. You have not quite gotten the knack of it. Try for a little common sense next time."

She gave a light laugh. "What on earth do you mean? Why should I try to hide it if I had a lady friend calling?"

"I haven't the faintest idea. Unless the lady should have been the duke's sister, acting as go-between."

This token show of jealousy pleased her. "You are too foolish, Dauntry," she said.

"Now, tell me what the constable had to say. Or have you been to the village yet?"

"He said there have been no strange men spotted in or about the village. No one else has been burgled. I met Beau on my way back. He and I plan to guard the dower house tonight, as you are not eager to come to the castle."

"No, that is not a good idea," she said at once. There was too much chance of his spotting Antonia.

Dauntry's first dash of surprise was fast turning to annoyance.

Cressida was hatching a different plan with regard to his sister. It was clear as crystal Antonia was in love with her Harold, and his efforts to find her suggested that the love was returned. To save them from embarrassment, she meant to find Harold and help the two of them to continue on their way to the Lake District without anyone's being aware of their imbroglio.

Dauntry said stiffly, "You have some aversion to my being here?"

"You will want to be looking for that letter, Dauntry. With three footmen and a dog and Beau, we shall be quite safe. As you said yourself, Tory knows who the man is and that he means no harm. Did you get a dog?"

"We have three, plus a pack of hunting

hounds, at the castle. I brought Tony's spaniel. I thought you might enjoy Sandy's company, as I hope he will enjoy yours. He has been skulking about like a lost soul since she left. I'll introduce you."

He called to Muffet before Cressida could stop him. Within seconds a golden sand colored spaniel came bolting in, barking excitedly, ears flopping. He had picked up his mistress's scent. He ran to her cup and began sniffing at it, knocking the cup over in his eagerness to find her.

The tea sloshed into the saucer, revealing half an inch of sugar in the bottom of the cup.

"Good gracious! The beast has no manners! Get him out of here," Cressida said. "Muffet!"

Muffet removed the unruly animal with great difficulty, for Sandy did not wish to leave.

"Strange," Dauntry said, frowning. "He is usually very docile. You can keep him outside. He is a good guard dog."

"That might be best."

They resumed their taking of tea, but between Cressida's nervousness and Dauntry's pique, it was not a great success. The instant he set down his teacup, Cressida rose. Dauntry rose politely. She began nudging him toward the door. "Don't let me keep you, Dauntry. It is of the utmost importance that you find that letter."

"Why do I get the feeling you wish to be rid of me? It cannot be that hand on my back, propelling me toward the door."

She pulled her hand away but continued moving toward the hallway, where Muffet was still struggling with the recalcitrant spaniel. Sandy escaped and ran to Dauntry, who tried to hold him, but he was off, down the hallway, barking and baying, with his leash hanging behind him. He turned at the door to the library, tail wagging fiercely.

"You had best see to him, Muffet," Cressida said nervously.

"He's picked up the scent of your intruder!" Dauntry said, and took a step after the dog.

Tory came bustling out of the library, pulling Sandy by his leash, and closed the door behind her. She cast a pleading look at Cressida, who understood that Antonia was hiding in the library.

"Oh, your lordship. You have brought Sandy to visit us. How nice," Tory said. "He seems pretty excited, does he not?"

Sandy was sniffing and scratching at the library door. "We'd best get him outside, your ladyship. What must that knock-in-the-cradle of a Jennet do but bring a baby rabbit into the house. You know how she loves animals. The creature seems to be an orphan. She has put a dish of lettuce in the library to feed it. I'll make her get rid of it as soon as we get the dog out of the way."

Jennet, curious at the racket above stairs, came running up from the kitchen. "That rabbit of yours is causing a great fuss, Jennet," Tory scolded.

"What rabbit?" Jennet asked.

"She hasn't the wits God gave a kitten, poor child. She has gone and forgotten all about it," Tory explained before turning a wrathful eye to Jennet. "I asked you to watch the ragout while I came up to see your rabbit was not nibbling the book bindings," Tory scolded, and taking the girl by the arm, began propelling her back down the kitchen stairs, while pulling at Sandy's leash with the other hand.

Cressida knew she was lying and thanked providence for the woman's quick imagination. Dauntry cast a long, searching gaze on Cressida. "At least Jennet remembered to remove your sprigged muslin before returning to the kitchen," he said satirically.

"Oh, yes, indeed. She is very careful."

"For a moonling."

"Don't let me detain you," Cressida said,

and began once more to maneuver Dauntry out the door.

"I thought we might go for a ride this afternoon," he said, digging in his heels and stopping.

"Oh, no, I could not possibly. I shall be very busy." She tugged at his arm.

"I am free for dinner, if you would like to join me or even if you would like me to join you."

"You would not care for Tory's ragout."

"Try me. I do not care for this ragout of lies and evasions I am being fed, but I am in no hurry to leave. I feel like Sandy, the way you are yanking me about."

"I can see you are in no hurry!" she said in exasperation.

"On the other hand, I can take a hint when I am hit over the head with it. Good day, Lady deCourcy."

He left, not in the best of tempers, and Cressida ran to the library. Antonia was not in evidence, but when Cressida saw only a pair of ladies' slippers from her crouching position under the table, she came out.

"Where is Sandy?" Antonia asked. "I am so happy he is here. May he come in, Lady deCourcy?"

"Of course, but first we must talk. Have you any idea where Harold is?"

Antonia pouted. "Somewhere, drunk as a lord," she said.

"He has visited this house twice. He must be close by."

"He would not be at home. I don't think he would dare to show his face in Beachy Head. If Melbury were here, I should think he would be with him, but Melbury was going to Bath."

"He has to eat. I wonder if he is hiding out at home. Is there a dower house at his estate?"

"Yes, but his aunt Gertrude is living there, and he would never hide at her house. She is horrid."

After a moment she added, "Who might know is Allan Brewster. He is Harold's best friend."

"I don't think Brewster knows a thing. I have spoken to him more than once. He thought my caller was Melbury."

"But if we could speak to Brewster, he might know where Harold is, for they are very good friends," Antonia said.

"Very well, then, we shall write to Brewster and ask him to call."

"But don't tell him I am here."

Cressida dashed off a note asking Brewster to call as soon as possible. It was close to lunchtime. They had either to take Miss

Wantage into their confidence, or continue to keep Antonia hidden.

"She is bound to find out sooner or later," Cressida said. "We might as well tell her."

Before lunch, Cressida had Miss Wantage and Beau called to the saloon to meet Lady Harold. Beau was favorably impressed by her beauty and averred that Lord Harold must have rocks in his head, by Jove. Miss Wantage was so thrilled at this scandalous story that she could hardly decide what tack to take. It was an excellent opportunity for lectures and condemnation of drunkenness and the morals of the younger generation. On the other hand, Lady Harold would be a countess when Lord Harold came into his honors, and it was well to have another house to visit.

"Poor child," she said, taking Antonia to her bosom. "What a wretched time you have had, and no one to turn to. If only I had known! Fancy them keeping you locked in the attic like a dog. Why, if the house had happened to catch fire, you would have been baked alive up there. Lord Harold wants a sound thrashing. If I were a man, I would give him one. Poor girl."

It was enough to send Antonia off into fresh bouts of self-pity. Other details of her ordeal came out. She had had to walk the five miles from Beachy Head in the dark, and someone — probably a dangerous murderer, or perhaps it was only a dog — had stalked her the whole way. She had blisters on both heels and had nearly died of starvation, for she hadn't enough money to buy food.

"We must get this child to bed at once and call the doctor, Cressida," Miss Wantage decreed. "What were you thinking of, not to have those wounds on her poor feet attended to? If they became infected, she might be crippled for life."

"They are very sore!" Antonia said, although she had not mentioned them before, or displayed any propensity to limp.

Miss Wantage herded her upstairs and put her to bed. She had their meals served on a tray, thus allowing Beau and Cressida a peaceful luncheon.

"The chit sounds a perfect ninnyhammer," Beau decided. "Naturally, Lord Harold was nervous as a tick on his wedding night. I daresay I should be the same. She is spoiled rotten, if you want my opinion. A pretty little thing, though."

"She has no experience, Beau. We should not be too hard on her."

"I would not be too hard on Lord Harold. Only look what she has put him through, all his masquerades — and where has he been laying his head while she is in your attic as snug as a bug in a rug? Probably curled up in some tree trunk or cave, like a dashed bear."

The afternoon dragged by slowly, as time does when one is waiting for something. Miss Wantage and Lady Harold never stirred from the bedroom. When Cressida went upstairs, she found them both sound asleep; Antonia in the bed and Miss Wantage in the chair, with her mouth hanging open and mild snorts issuing from it. It seemed best to leave them thus. At dinnertime there was still no reply from Mr. Brewster.

Cressida and Beau were just leaving the dinner table when there was a knock on the door, and Muffet came to announce Mr. Brewster.

Chapter Fifteen

"Good evening, milady," Brewster said with a bow he had practiced ten times in front of the mirror before leaving home. It was a very model of elegance, and he was extremely annoyed that Beau should destroy it by choosing that moment to walk into the saloon and capsize him in mid-bow.

"Sorry," Beau said, setting Mr. Brewster back on an even keel.

The incident upset Brewster to such a degree that he forgot the apology he had memorized and said with a scowl, "Sorry I am so late in coming. What must Mama do but take into her head she wanted to visit Mrs. Peabody, who lives halfway to Brighton, and, of course, I got stuck to accompany her. If your note is about Melbury, he is back right enough, but he only landed in last night around ten and has not left my place since. He admits he had a word with Tory at your kitchen door before coming to me, but she would not let him in."

This explained Tory's positive assertion that Melbury was in the neighborhood, but that was not why Lady deCourcy had summoned Brewster. She opened her budget to him.

Brewster listened, then spoke. "So this is where she has run to ground. Harold will be vastly relieved to hear it. He has run me ragged these two days looking for her. The fact is, he called on me for assistance the evening of the day we met in Beachy Head, ma'am. Looked like a turf cutter, with a couple of days' growth of beard and his jacket as black as — well, he had been sleeping in a barn. And it was a very good jacket, too. Stutz."

"Then he is with you!" Cressida exclaimed.

"Devil a bit of it. There was no way of hiding him and getting him cleaned up without the nosy-Parker servants discovering it. What we did, we eased open a window and slid him into Melbury's place, as Melbury was away at Bath. That is why Melbury is staying with me now. I did not want him to learn Harold is at Cove House, or he would cause some sort of mischief. Harold has been lying low during the day and prowling about at night looking for his good woman." He turned to Beau, adding, "He is sorry about that knock on the skull, Montgomery. Hope it hasn't shaken a brain loose."

"It was loose already. You have only to ask Sid."

"Sid who?"

"Lady deCourcy's name is Cressida. Sid, for short."

"Ah. Charming," he said with a frown that denoted disapproval of the name. "Er, about Sissie —"

"Sissie who?" Beau asked.

"Harold's wife, Tony. Antonia. I don't see why all the ladies are using men's names this year. Dashed confusing. Will Tony see him? I have a note here from him making his apologies for the monumental disaster of the treacle moon. I wish she will see him, for I am running out of excuses to keep Melbury from going home. Besides, Harold is trying to dump the whole fiasco in my dish, if you please. I told him, one tot of brandy to relax. What must the gudgeon do but gargle down a cupful. Nervous as a martyr at the stake, of course, staving off the moment. Can hardly blame him. Feels a dashed fool, and so he is. Anyhow, he is a reformed character, so if you would give Sissie this billet doux —" He handed Cressida a grimy note, folded in four.

"Leave it to Melbury not to have any decent stationery," he said. "Harold scribbled this on the back of a bill or some such thing.

Let us hope Sissie has the sense to have him back, for she will never hear the end of it from all the old cats in the neighborhood if she don't."

"I shall give her the note myself," Cressida said, and ran off to deliver it.

In the rose guest chamber, Miss Wantage guarded the young bride. Sandy lolled at her feet. He batted his tail on the floor to welcome Cressida. Miss Wantage lifted a finger to her lips. "Shhh! I have just got her to sleep."

Cressida held up the letter and said in a whisper, "Good news. This note is from her husband. He wants to come and make it up with her."

"The villain!" Miss Wantage charged. "We must not let her go. You will not credit what the beast put her through, Cressida. Drunkenness, common brawling in a public room, arrest — all this on his wedding night, if you please, while his innocent bride waited, trembling, for his return. She is well rid of him."

"I hope you have not been speaking to Antonia in this vein, giving her a disgust of her husband," Cressida said.

"I? How should I know what had happened? It is Lady Harold who told me. I merely agreed with her that she had married a scoundrel and must be rid of him at all costs."

"Lord Harold is not a scoundrel. He is a frightened boy who had a glass of false courage before going to his bride and fell into an argument."

"That will be for Lady Harold to decide," Miss Wantage declared. Sandy, as if sensing some argument, emitted one yelp and was silenced by Miss Wantage.

"So it will," Cressida said, and shook the lady's shoulder, despite Miss Wantage's dire warning that the consequences would be on her head.

Antonia's eyelids fluttered open, and she sat up. "Oh, Lady deCourcy. Is it morning already?"

"No, it is still evening. I have news for you — a letter from Lord Harold," she said, proffering the grimed paper. "He has been looking high and low for you."

Antonia snatched eagerly for the letter and opened it. Her face first turned bone white, then, as she read, a rosy flush suffused her cheeks and her eyes misted up.

Miss Wantage patted her shoulder consolingly. "There, there, my dear. You do not have to see him. We shall give you safe harbor here."

"Of course she will see him," Cressida

said. "He is her husband."

"In name only," Miss Wantage pointed out with a satisfied smile. "He had not had his way with her yet. It is not too late to undo the damage. She can have the marriage annulled."

Antonia was already scrambling out of bed, with Sandy leaping at her in an ill-bred manner. "You are very kind, Miss Wantage, but I think I ought to see Harold, for he is so very sorry and miserable without me."

"They can all string a good line when they have to," Miss Wantage warned. "Remember his drunkenness and brawling — and that on the honeymoon, when he was on his best behavior. One trembles to think how he will behave later."

Antonia looked unhappy. "Harold does not usually drink too much, and is really very behaved as a rule. He was just nervous, you see."

"Is that what you will have to put up with every time your lord and master chooses to be nervous?"

Cressida managed to hold on to her temper, but she saw she must be rid of Miss Wantage. "Miss Wantage," she said, "will you just check with Muffet and see that he has locked all the doors? We do not want a repeat of last night's trouble, and it is coming on dark."

Miss Wantage was always ready to put her own comfort and safety in front of anyone else's and was gotten rid of in this manner.

Antonia turned a pale face to her rescuer. "Do you think she is right, Lady de-Courcy? She is so much older and wiser. I know she has only my welfare at heart. She has been very kind to me but I do love Harold."

"Miss Wantage is indeed older, but she has never been in love, Antonia. If you want to end up like her —"

"Oh, no! I shall answer Harold's note telling him I understand. I think I did understand before, really, but was just miffed that he ruined our honeymoon. He says we will start all over."

"I shall give Brewster your note to deliver, and Harold can write back with the details of when he can come for you."

"Yes, that will be fine. And you will see that Sandy gets back to the castle until I return?"

"Of course."

Cressida kept a sharp eye on the door to see that Miss Wantage did not come bustling back to undo her work. Antonia scribbled off a note with many x's on the bottom, folded it, and gave it to Cressida for delivery.

"I shall get dressed again to be ready for him," she said. "If you could just send your woman to assist me, Lady deCourcy."

"I shall send Jennet."

"That will be fine. I do like Jennet. She is very good with coiffures."

Cressida took the note to Mr. Brewster.

"I know Harold is dead eager to get on with it," he said. "To save coming back, I believe I can take a guess when he will be here. Twenty minutes for me to get to Melbury's place, an hour for Harold to get himself cleaned up and get the rig harnessed, a half an hour to return, and there you are. Say two hours in round figures, for you may be sure some little thing will go wrong to hold him up."

"He won't want to drive his carriage about the neighborhood, will he?" Beau asked. "In case someone recognizes it, I mean."

"No one will get a good look at it at night," Brewster replied. "I shall tell him to leave it at the main road, for the servants from the castle would recognize it, and it makes a grant thundering racket on that pebbled drive. Harold will come on foot up the drive. Can you have Sissie ready in two hours, Lady deCourcy?"

Lady deCourcy would have agreed to have

her ready in two minutes. She wanted the girl out of the house before Miss Wantage could get at her again. She agreed. Brewster made another of his exquisite bows, uninterrupted this time, and left.

"We can no longer complain of long, boring evenings," Beau said, smiling. "It is like an elopement, with the romance and the secrecy and all. By Jove, I think I shall elope — if I can ever find any lady foolish enough to have me."

"It will be tricky getting Antonia smuggled out when we have three of Dauntry's footmen guarding the doors," was Cressida's reply. "I shall suggest that she leave before they get here. She can wait for Harold on the main road. Of course, she cannot go alone. We should accompany her. Actually, I am curious to meet Lord Harold."

"Sounds a bit of a nig-nog to me."

Miss Wantage soon joined them. "Muffet has all doors secured," she announced, and soon turned the conversation to the more interesting topic.

"It is strange Lord Harold did not come in person to deliver that grimy old letter," she averred. "It was so filthy, I hated to see her touch it. I daresay he is foxed. I don't know how Lady Dauntry could have handed that innocent child over to such a villain.

And where is Lady Harold's chaperon during all this melee?"

"She would hardly take a chaperon on a wedding trip," Beau said.

"Her dresser, then. Lady Dauntry ought not to have sent the child all the way to the Lake District without any female companion."

"That is the way I should like to travel on my honeymoon," Cressida said.

"But you are hardly a young girl, my dear. Certainly a lady of your age need not fear being meddled with by men — though you really ought to have had Crump put a lock on your door while he was here, for there is no saying where a ravening lunatic will strike. Well now, what shall we do this evening? Would you like a game of Pope Joan? Not for money, of course. I don't approve of playing cards for money, but just for the sport of the game."

"Where is the sport if you cannot pocket a few sous?" Beau said, and picked up a journal.

Miss Wantage delivered a few homilies on the vice of gambling. Before she had finished, they were interrupted by a knock on the door. E'er long, Muffet showed Lord Dauntry in.

Cressida looked at him with vexation in

every line of her body. As if a footman at every door were not enough! How the devil was she to get Antonia smuggled out with Dauntry sitting in her saloon?

"I did not see Sandy about," he said after curt greetings had been exchanged.

"He is upstairs, patrolling the hall," Cressida replied. "Can I help you, Dauntry?"

"A glass of wine would not go amiss."

That was not her meaning, but she was obliged to pour him a glass of wine. She had hoped to discover what he wanted, do it quickly, and be rid of him.

Miss Wantage was just suggesting a game of Pope Joan, when Sandy was heard in the hallway. Fearing that Antonia was not far behind, since she did not know of her brother's arrival, Cressida jumped up and dashed into the hall.

"Tell Lady Harold her brother is here," she whispered to Muffet, whom she had taken into her confidence. "And put the dog out, Muffet."

"His lordship told me he has stationed his three footmen around the doors. How are you to get the lassie smuggled out, missy?"

"She is not due to leave for nearly two hours. I shall be rid of Dauntry long before that. We shall have to distract a footman while she leaves."

She returned in a flurried state to find Miss Wantage drawing a deck of cards out of her sewing box.

"Now that we are four, we can have a few hands of whist," she announced. "Lord Dauntry prefers whist to Pope Joan."

Miss Wantage could drag a game of whist out for hours. "I do not feel like cards this evening," Cressida said. "In fact, I have a slight migraine." She looked hopefully at her caller, to see if this got him from his seat.

Dauntry was looking a question at her. He had sensed a lack of warmth in her greeting, and wondered at it. He began to outline where he had placed each footman, and how they were to patrol the house by turn, with Sandy prowling loose as well.

"Let us check the windows as well, to be perfectly safe," he said with a sapient look to Cressida.

She sensed that he wished to be alone with her, but was so eager for him to leave that she ignored it. "Muffet has checked the windows," she replied.

"You recall the misunderstanding about the library door the night Tory went up to the castle," Miss Wantage reminded her. "It might be a good idea to just check the library and see she has not left it ajar again. There is no counting on servants to do anything."

Before Cressida could object, Dauntry rose and held out a commanding hand to her. She rose stiffly to accompany him.

As they walked toward the library, he said, "Have I accidentally stumbled into the ice house instead of the dower house?"

"It has been a trying day," she said, and opened the library door into a dark room.

Dauntry found the tinderbox and lit two lamps. Cressida went to check the handle of the door and gave a shriek of alarm. A pair of close-set eyes peered in through the glass of the French doors, giving her a fright. Dauntry was immediately behind her, his arms protectively around her shoulders.

"It is Gaunt, my footman," he said. "You really are a bundle of nerves tonight. I told you he was there." Gaunt nodded and moved away from the door into the shadows.

Dauntry turned her around to face him, still holding on to her shoulders. "Is it just fear of the intruder that upsets you?" he asked, gazing at her with shadowed eyes.

"I have other things on my mind," she said distractedly.

"Other things, or other people?"

She gave a guilty start. Did he know Antonia was here? "What do you mean?" she asked nervously.

"To be more precise, I mean another person. Specifically, the duke."

"The duke?" she asked, surprised. "I have not given him a thought since coming here."

His harsh features softened to pleasure. "Well, that is some small consolation at least. Cressida, I think you know —"

She heard a sound at the doors leading outside, and glancing at them, she saw Sandy pawing the glass, while the footman attempted to pull him away.

Dauntry had come determined to speak, but between the unexpected audience and the lady's state of distraction, he found it uphill work. He took a deep breath to make one more effort.

"I think you know how I feel about you," he said.

Cressida could not like his timing, but she felt a jolt of pleasure jar her heart. Her lips trembled open, and she gazed at him expectantly. His hands slid down from her shoulders to draw her into his arms.

"Well now!" an exasperated voice announced from the doorway into the corridor. Turning, they saw Tory squinting her eyes at them. "I can see I came at a bad time," she said with an apologetic glance at her mistress, "but there is a bit of trouble above stairs, milady."

"What sort of trouble?" Cressida asked.

Antonia! What could have happened to her?

"No need to get into a fit, milady, if I could just have a moment of your time. It is about Sandy. Hasn't he gone and chewed the toe out of a blue kid slipper."

"Surely that can wait until later," Dauntry said at his most daunting.

Tory fixed her mistress with a commanding eye. "How is a lady to go out with only one slipper?"

It was Antonia's slipper that had been destroyed, then. She was preparing for flight and had no other shoes to wear.

She gave Dauntry a conning smile. "You quite underestimate the importance of a lady's slippers, milord. I shall come at once, Tory."

"I knew I did not stand high in your estimation, but I had not thought an old shoe took precedence over —"

"But they were my very favorite slippers. Do not let me detain you, Dauntry. I am sure you have more important things to do. We shall be quite safe with your footmen. Good night."

"I shall make a tour of the house and return — after you have tended to your slipper."

On this angry speech he went out.

"I'm that sorry, milady, for I can see you

are making great time with his lordship," Tory said, "but Lady Antonia — I ought to call her Lady Harold, but never mind. She has flown into a fit of tears about her shoe. We tried a pair of yours — I knew you would not begrudge her one pair when you have nine sitting in your room — but she could put both her dainty little feet into one of yours. She says she cannot go barefoot on her wedding trip, and who shall blame her? Miss Wantage's are even larger, and us servants have nothing fine enough for a lady."

"Send Jennet to the castle to bring a pair of Antonia's own slippers down here. The cook there knows she is here."

"The very thing. But Jennet is busy trying to keep Lady Antonia's wailing down to a roar. I'll send the backhouse boy."

"And I shall try to think of some excuse to be rid of Dauntry. It is clear we will never get Antonia bounced off while he is here."

"You must do it, but do it gentle. His lordship has a bit of a temper. Used to getting his own way."

"Yes, I had noticed," Cressida said.

"While you are in spirits, milady, I have a confession to make. Circumstances obliged me to tell you a small white lie. About counting the spoons after Lord Harold's visit — it was no such a thing. I wouldn't want you to think him light-fingered. It was to make you believe he was Melbury, you see. I knew you'd learn his little ways sooner or later. The untruth has been bothering me," she said piously.

"I quite understand, Tory," Cressida said, and went upstairs.

Chapter Sixteen

Cressida found Antonia in the rose guest chamber, examining a well-chewed slipper. She held it up to show her hostess when she entered. "Oh, milady, only see what Sandy has done. Did Tory tell you?"

"Indeed she did. Tory has sent in secret to the castle for another pair of slippers. Dauntry was here, and may be returning, so you must be very careful not to come downstairs. He has posted footmen at all the doors as well."

"Why do you need a footman at the doors? You have a butler."

"It is because of Lord Harold's breaking in last night. He gave us quite a fright."

Antonia giggled. "Fancy anyone guarding the doors against Harold! His head will be big as a pumpkin when I tell him. Now that you know it was only Harold, you do not require the guards at the doors."

"That is true," Cressida replied, "but if I turn them off, Dauntry will want to know why, and you do not want him to know Harold and you are back."

"You must not tell him! We would never hear the end of it. But how am I to get away unseen, with footmen who have known me forever standing guard?" she asked, her lower lip already quivering in disappointment.

"We shall create a diversion at one of the doors to distract the footman. Beau will make some fuss. Best to do it before Dauntry returns, I think. You slip out while Beau keeps the footman busy. Beau will meet you and take you to the edge of the road to wait for Harold."

The quivering lip steadied just before lifting in a smile. "How exciting! It is just like an elopement."

Cressida encouraged this mood. The poor girl would have a longish wait, and needed the excitement to keep up her spirits.

While awaiting the delivery of the slippers, Antonia had Jennet pack her bandbox. As soon as the slippers arrived, she put them on and crept to the head of the staircase to await her escape.

Below stairs, Beau and Cressida met to discuss the matter. To escape Miss Wantage, who was bound to put in her oar and create difficulties, they went to the library, pretending to discuss sailing. Other than condemning the yacht wholesale as a monstrous waste of money and an invitation to drowning, Miss Wantage took no interest in it. It was arranged that Beau would go out for a stroll, leaving by the library door, and letting the footman see him. When he got beyond Gaunt's view, he would shout and thrash about, pretending he had been attacked, to draw Gaunt from the door to his rescue. Antonia would then slip out unseen, hide in the bushes, and wait for Beau to join her.

"Gaunt will be with me by then. I shall have to continue my stroll after being attacked. I am a brave soul," Beau said, "venturing back out into the night after being set upon by a band of thugs."

"You are right. No one would believe it," Cressida said, frowning.

"Thank you very much!"

"No, it will not fadge, Beau. I must slip out with Antonia and accompany her down to the main road to wait for Harold while you distract Gaunt."

"What if Dauntry comes back asking for you?"

"Tell him I have gone to bed with a headache. I have already complained of one."

"But that leaves two ladies waiting on the roadside an hour in the dark, and you are left all alone to return from the main road after Antonia leaves. Better for you to go out

233

and make the racket to distract Gaunt, and I shall slip out with Antonia and accompany her to wait for Harold."

"I believe you are right. Yes, that is what we will do. The only problem is how I am to get out of the house to create this racket. I can hardly go out for a stroll alone at night. I need an excuse."

"You shall require a breath of air, we go out together, I shall say I want to blow a cloud and walk Gaunt a little away from the door, you run beyond sight and holler. When we run to your aid, Antonia sneaks out. You blushingly admit you was scared by your own shadow and nip back inside. I go on for my stroll to finish my cigar, and meet up with Antonia."

"Yes, and we shall extinguish the lamps in the library to keep the doorway nice and dark. I shall wear a dark mantle as well."

Cressida thought about it a moment, envisaging the scene in her head, then said, "It begins to sound like a French farce. All we require is a few more doors and some lovers to hide behind them. Never mind, it will have to do."

They went over their plan a few times, Cressida got her dark mantle, then had Antonia smuggled down to the library, where they had extinguished the lights so Gaunt could not see in. The plan began auspiciously enough, although the darkness outside was a little frightening when they first stepped out. As her eyes became accustomed to the dark, Cressida could see the park spreading before her, spotted with darker shadows that were trees and bushes. A pale white moon looked down from the black heavens. The breeze from the sea was chilly.

Beau offered Gaunt a cigar, and they stepped off a few paces to protect Lady deCourcy from the smoke. She began to walk away from the house into the park, toward the shadowed concealment of the spreading elm, where she stopped. No, she must go a little farther, though it really was rather frightening. The library door was easily distinguishable from there, if Gaunt should chance to look. The leaves above, stirred by the breeze, emitted a menacing hiss.

She was just about to continue, when a form came lunging out from behind the tree to attack her. She felt her arms being seized and pulled roughly behind her. Fear jolted her heart, momentarily holding her speechless with terror. Who could it be? Was it Harold, come early? No, he could not be here yet. She couldn't see her attacker, who was behind her, but she felt the rough strength in his hands and arms. Her heart banged in her throat.

She was just summoning breath and courage to shout, when the strong hands on her arms suddenly loosened their grip. Why had he let her go? She emitted one ear-splitting scream, then jerked away and began to run. Her attacker grabbed the tail of her mantle and pulled her back roughly.

"Cressida?" the man asked in an incredulous voice.

She recognized that voice. Interning to peer over her shoulder, she saw the unmistakable form of Lord Dauntry. While still digesting this unwelcome fact, she heard running footsteps, and soon Beau and Gaunt were at her side. She cast one quick peek at the library doors and saw a dark form slip out. Antonia did not realize the scream was genuine, that Dauntry was there. It might still work. Antonia had escaped unseen.

"What the devil is going on?" Dauntry demanded. "Cressida, why are you out alone at night? What is the point of my guarding the house if you choose to leave it? If I had been a ken smasher, I might have killed you."

Her mind went temporarily blank. She just stared at Dauntry with guilt writ large on her face. Fortunately, Beau came to her rescue.

"Why, she was not alone, milord. We came

out together. Sid had a migraine, wanted a breath of air. I came out with her. I was just blowing a cloud with Gaunt, not two steps away."

"You are not paid to blow a cloud, Gaunt, but to protect Lady deCourcy's house," Dauntry said angrily.

"My fault, milord. I gave him the cigar," Beau said. "How is the migraine, Sid? Feeling better now, I hope?"

"Much better," she said foolishly, swallowing a gulp.

Behind Dauntry's back, Beau winked. Cressida assumed he had also seen Antonia leave the library. "I think you can go back inside now," he said. "Dashed foolish of you to wander off into the dark, Sid. You ought to have waited for me. I was just asking Gaunt if there had been any action. Quiet as the grave out here, he tells me. That is a good thing, eh?"

At this point, Sandy, who had been patrolling the house, caught his mistress's scent and went howling past in pursuit, as if she were a long-lost bone.

"Chasing a rabbit, very likely," Beau said. "Well, I shall continue my stroll, help Gaunt keep an eye on things. Why don't you take Lord Dauntry inside, Sid? Give him a glass of wine."

Dauntry realized he had stumbled into the middle of an imbroglio and fully expected Cressida would find an excuse to be rid of him. To his astonishment, she gave a weak, guilty smile and latched on to his arm.

"Yes, do come inside, Dauntry. I am still a little shaken. You run along, Beau. I shan't let Dauntry attack you," she added, beginning to recover. The house was the best place for him until Beau and Antonia got safely away.

Beau went whistling off into the darkness. When Sandy's barks turned to yelps of delight, Cressida knew he had met up with his mistress. She drew Dauntry toward the library, chatting brightly. "You gave me quite a turn, Dauntry, lurking in the park like a hedgebird. I hope that is not a regular habit."

"Not at all," he said, holding the library door for her to enter. "Why are the lights extinguished? I collect you and Beau left from the library, as the doors are open?"

"It is much easier to see out the window if the lamps are not lit. We were on the qui vive for the intruder," she explained.

Dauntry busied himself with relighting the lamps. "I assume Miss Wantage is still occupying the saloon?"

"Very likely. Would you care for a few

hands of Pope Joan?" They exchanged a speaking glance.

"Or we could remain here."

"If you like."

"We would not want to scandalize Saint Wantage. I fancy the tale you are about to tell me is not fit for delicate ears," Dauntry said.

"Tale? Why, whatever can you mean, Dauntry?" she asked, assuming an air of nonchalance.

"I am not a cretin, Cressida. It is clear to the meanest intelligence that you are running some rig."

"You have a poor opinion of me!"

"On the contrary, I have a high opinion of your pluck and intelligence, to say nothing of your powers of dissimulation. It is hardly your fault if Tony and Harold have made egregious asses of themselves. Now, tell me what happened."

"Tony?" she asked in a weak voice. "Harold? What — why should you leap to the conclusion it has anything to do with them? They are on their way north, are they not?"

"I think not. I was not certain that green and white skirt I saw fleeing your saloon was Tony's, though it looked familiar. I thought the surfeit of sugar in the cup might possibly have been Jennet's doing,

239

though Tony has the same revolting habit. It was not until Brewster's flying visit this evening that I became fairly sure what was afoot. Sandy's joyful yelps merely confirmed it. Then when I recalled Sandy's love of shoes, there was no longer any possibility of doubt. Have Tony and Harold run into a muddle so soon? What happened, were they robbed, thus cutting short the honeymoon?"

"I don't know what you are talking about. Brewster has been promising to call ever since I met him."

"Very likely, but a gent don't make his first call after dinner in the evening. And why did he head north instead of going home when he left?"

"Have you been spying on me?"

"Use your wits! Of course I have. Are Harold and Tony putting up at Melbury's place? Why the devil did she not just write me to send her money?"

"You are quite mistaken — about everything."

"Am I mistaken that Beau saw a blond lady at the cottage? Good God! Don't tell me Tony has left her bridegroom, after pestering me to death to let her marry him!" He read the astonishment on her face. "So that's it!"

"You must not be angry with her, Dauntry. It was not all her fault by a long chalk."

"I agree it takes two to create a quarrel. What was his part in it? You might as well tell me, or I shall suspect only the worst. Surely to God it was not another woman?"

"No! How can you say such a thing? It was an excess of brandy on their wedding night. He fell into an argument below stairs at the inn."

"Mawworm! She would have forgiven him if he had asked her nicely."

"Unfortunately, he was in no position to do so."

"Drank himself into a stupor, did he?" Dauntry asked, his lips moving in amusement.

"Worse. Drank himself into the roundhouse. She didn't know what to do and came home."

Dauntry just shook his head in frustration. "She lacks your venturesome spirit. I wager Lady deCourcy would not turn tail and run in such a circumstance."

"Indeed I would run — to the roundhouse to ring a peal over the constable. She behaved very foolishly, but she is young, and so is Harold. They have made up their differences and hoped to get away again before you — anyone — knew what had happened."

"So I am to feature as the ogre in this Cheltenham farce, am I?"

"Yes," she said bluntly, "and I wish you will pretend to be in ignorance of the whole thing, Dauntry, for it is exceedingly humiliating for them."

"I am not likely to broadcast such a jape about my own family. The foolish chit ought to have come to me. There is no excuse for her battening herself on you, no doubt causing a deal of mischief."

"She was no trouble at all — once I knew who she was. It was the confusion of things disappearing, and noises in the attic, and trays being taken to the cottage. It was Harold who caused more trouble, pretending to be Melbury, and breaking into my room last night. Tory added her bit, lying her head off."

"Now, there is a clear case of the pot calling the kettle black. You are no stranger to lies yourself, madam."

"I promised to help Tony. A few minor evasions seemed a small price to pay."

"As my sister would not think to thank you, may I now tender my appreciation for your efforts on her behalf? I think Tony might have come to her brother with her problem. And you, shrew, might have come to your landlord."

"Speaking of lies, and landlords . . ."

"You know my excuse — er, reason. That missing letter could prove vital. The safety of England must come above all else."

"I am not an ogre either, milord. You might have told me the truth. Now that all is out in the open, I have a recommendation to make. Take those three unnecessary footmen, send them to the cottage, and tear the place apart until you find the letter."

"I shall send them home. The letter will not be found buried beneath a floor, or between the joints of a wall." He went to the door and gave Gaunt the word that the footmen could leave.

"Tell me all about Tony and Harold's tribulations. I could use a good laugh," he said, settling himself comfortably on the sofa.

She told the story as she knew it, from the first night when Miss Wantage had heard noises in the attic, through Tory's insisting it was bats, Antonia being hustled from attic to cottage and back again when Dauntry spent so much time at the cottage looking for the letter.

"She has given you a poor notion of the

intelligence of the Dauntrys," he said.

"Not in the least. I already had a poor opinion of the Dauntrys' intelligence before I met her. How you could think I wanted to hire the dower house when I said specifically the little Swiss cottage on the cliff is beyond me. I think you misunderstood on purpose."

"Now, that, my dear, is an extremely provocative statement to make to an unexceptionable gentleman."

"Unexceptionable! You have a high opinion of yourself, for a liar!"

Miss Wantage exploded into the room like Jehovah. "Cressida! Really, this is the outside of enough. As if entertaining a gentleman alone were not bad enough, you have to revile him, after all his kindness to us. It is small wonder you are still single at your age."

Dauntry rose, trying to maintain some shred of civility. "Mere persiflage, madam. No offense was taken, I promise you."

"You are foolishly generous, milord. To forgive such behavior is tantamount to encouraging it. But I did not come here to ring a peal over Lady deCourcy, for she told me she and Beau were going to the library to study his yacht." An edge of suspicion tinged her voice as she turned back to Cressida.

"How did you get rid of Beau? Is he in on this tryst as well? Corrupting a minor along with all the rest!"

"Beau stepped out to blow a cloud," Cressida said through clenched lips.

"A filthy habit." Miss Wantage turned her gimlet gaze back to Dauntry. "I did not see you come in. Very odd, as I never left the saloon until I came here. You must have sneaked in by the library door."

"I entered by the library door, if it is of any interest whatsoever to you."

"I am Lady deCourcy's chaperon. Naturally, her carrying on with a gentleman she feels obliged to term a liar is of interest to me." She turned her back pointedly on Dauntry and said to Cressida, "You will never get a decent husband carrying on in this way, miss. You will do nothing but lose whatever remains of your reputation, which is not much, from what I hear."

"You are mistaken," Dauntry said, his nostrils pinching dangerously. "Lady deCourcy already has a husband — if she wants him."

Miss Wantage stood silent a moment, then, without offering either apologies or congratulations, she said, "I came here to inform you that those footmen his lordship sent over have ran off and left

245

us unprotected, Cressida. Like master, like servant."

On this leveler, she turned and stalked off.

"So there," Dauntry said, and resumed his seat.

Chapter Seventeen

The air of discomfort in the library was not all due to Miss Wantage's outburst, but it was of this that Cressida spoke.

"I should go and speak to her," she said.

"It is for Miss Wantage to apologize to you. After her behavior, I should give her her congé, if she were in my employ."

"But she is not a servant, Dauntry. She is one of those removed cousins, whatever that may be. In any case, she runs from relative to relative, retailing all the family gossip. I had best hang on to whatever vestige of my reputation I still have after this night's work."

"Nonsense! You have done nothing wrong. If society thinks you have, then I want you to know I was serious when I said you have a husband if you want one."

She looked for signs of romance, and saw only a scowling visage. A duty proposal, then, to protect her name. "I am gratified by the honor you do me."

"Don't talk such fustian!"

Cressida gave an impatient twitch and resumed her speech. "But despite the honor, I cannot —"

"Forget the honor. What is your answer?"

"Will you stop interrupting? I had a nice speech all ready, and you have made me lose my place."

"You were anticipating an offer, then?" he asked mischievously.

"During my years in London I have received a few offers. I have a standard speech prepared for such contingencies. I might have known Miss Wantage would shame you into offering eventually."

"I have no shame. Nor do I give a tinker's curse what that harpy says or does. The world must know her reputation by now. Never mind your set speech. I think you and I would deal admirably. I love you. Will you marry me?"

He was still scowling, but his eyes betrayed a different mood — of uncertainty, and hope.

"No! We should not deal admirably in the least. You only think you know me. I am not at all the sort of dasher you take me for, despite my reputation. I would not condone your using the cottage as your papa used it, for example. I know my friends make a joke of such things. Well, it is society's way. I can tolerate it in others, but never in my own husband."

"Then we are agreed on the basic principles — faithful till death do us part."

She peered at him from the side of her eyes. "From the way you are glaring at me, that will not be long."

"I am not glaring."

"You are so, ogre!"

His rough frown softened to a smile as he gazed into those glimmering emerald eyes. She sat, waiting in perfect stillness, like a cat who might permit herself to be stroked if he moved very carefully. He saw an untamed spirit trapped in the body of a beautiful lady with an exquisite face.

His arms reached for her. "Shrew!"

Her lips trembled into a smile as his lips seized hers and pressed them with a kiss. When she did not object, his arms tightened around her until the breath caught in her lungs, growing and expanding until she felt ready to burst. Her arms looped around his neck, with one hand gently palming his cheek. This was what had been missing with other gentlemen; this sense of wholeness, of finding the other half of herself, of peace. But it was a very exciting peace. As the kiss deepened, she forgot about the peace and merely tried to capture for all time this first ecstasy of loving, and being loved.

When he released her, they just gazed quietly at each other a moment with wildly dilated eyes.

"Is that a yes?" he asked in a husky voice.

"Yes, Dauntry. I will marry you, if you are sure —"

He seized her two hands and raised them to his hot lips. "I have never been surer of anything in my life."

"Then it is settled. Shall we tell Miss Wantage?"

"The hell with Miss Wantage," he said, and kissed her again.

At the sound of heavy footfalls beyond the door, they drew reluctantly apart, expecting to see Miss Wantage. It was Tory who came in, holding Antonia's soiled suit and one good slipper.

"I wonder now," she said while her eyes trotted all over the couple, who sat close together on the sofa. "Shall I just throw this old suit of yours into the dustbin, your ladyship, or will you be wanting to see if it can be rescued?" Her wandering eyes settled on Cressida in a commanding way. "It is all over dust and grime from that tumble you took from your mount the other day."

"Dustbin," Dauntry said. "The game is over, Tory. I know Tony was here, and if I did not, you may be sure I would recognize the suit she wore on her honeymoon. It was one of her chief concerns for a week."

"I'll just check the pockets, then," Tory said, unashamed at being caught dead to rights. "It would be a pity to throw out a good handkerchief or a bit of loose change."

She rifled through the pockets and drew out a crumpled bit of paper. "What is this?" she asked, frowning over it. "I cannot make heads or tails of it. It must be French, though it don't look quite like it either, all jumbled up with numbers. Some game she and Lord Harold were playing, very likely, before the gossoon went and drank hisself into a stupor."

She crumpled the paper up and was about to drop it in the wastebasket when Dauntry suddenly stiffened. "Let me see it," he said in an excited voice.

Tory handed it over. As he read it, a smile of triumph seized his swarthy face. "That will be all, Tory," he said.

"A pity about the slipper," she said, holding it out for their inspection. "It could be fixed up with little trouble."

"Thank you," Cressida said, and took it from her. "That will be all, Tory."

"Could I bring you a nice cup of tea?" Tory asked. Sensing some importance in the paper, she was inclined to linger.

"No, thank you," Dauntry said. "Just run along," he added when she still stood.

"I'll have a word with Old Muffet," she decided. "Very likely he could do with a cup, what with all the doings afoot."

On this cryptic speech, she left.

"What is it? Is it the letter?" Cressida asked.

"Yes. Tony must have picked it up when she was at the cottage. There is some of her scribbling on the back. It looks like the beginning of a note to Mama. 'Please don't tell Dauntry,' she has written." He frowned at that, but soon reverted to the letter.

"I must get this off to London at once. If I leave now, I can be back by tomorrow morning."

"Whatever you think, Dauntry. You will be careful." She placed a small white hand on his sleeve. "I should hate to lose you so soon. No one would ever believe I had an offer from you."

"I still can't believe you accepted." Holding up the letter, he said, "This is my lucky day. I have a distinct feeling all my days will be lucky from now on." Then he kissed her gently and left.

It was over an hour before Beau returned. Cressida awaited him in the saloon, since Miss Wantage had gone upstairs.

"Well, they are off on their second honey-moon," Beau said. "Lord Harold seems a nice sort when he is being himself. Now that we have gotten that pair sorted out, I can get busy full-time on the *Sea Dog*. You really must give it a try, Sid, or you will be bored to flinders. Oh, by the bye, you will need a new companion. I saw your carriage bowling down the road as I was coming home. Wantage drew to a stop, told me to tell you she will not stay in a house of ill repute. She will catch the stage to Bath in Beachy Head and send John Groom back with the carriage. I told her to take your rig to London, to make sure she don't make some excuse and come creeping back."

"She didn't even say good-bye!" Cressida said. "She must have left while I was in the library with Dauntry."

"Very likely. How did you get rid of her?"

"She went into a pelter when she saw Dauntry in the library, accused him of sneaking in for immoral purposes."

"Good God! You will be firmly established as a scarlet woman by the time she is through with you."

"I must count on my husband to redeem my reputation," she said, and told Beau about her engagement.

"Ah, so you have brought him up to

scratch. Good work. Wish you happy and all that rot. You want to get shackled right away, before Wantage changes her mind and comes scrambling back to pester you. I daresay Lady Dauntry — the dowager, I mean — won't be wanting the dower house until autumn. I shall stay on here with my *Sea Dog*. I wonder if Hanson and Tory would like to come down and join me. We could have some races."

When he began to speak of reefed mainsails and trysails and other nautical matters, Cressida just sat, letting the meaningless wards flow over her as she thought of the future. How very strange life was. All those months in London looking about for a match, only to find the perfect one when she had stopped looking.

She excused herself and went to tell Muffet. A few moments later, Tory came sidling into the saloon, wearing a broad smile.

"Congratulations, milady. Old Muffet just told me the news. I have been thinking over matters, for I have an eye in my head to see which way the wind was blowing, as you might say. Lady Dauntry always planned to move into the dower house here when his lordship chose a bride. She will be bringing Eaton, her butler, with her, so I fancy you will take Old Muffet along to the castle to finish out his few years there. That being the case, I wonder if you would put in a word with her ladyship about me taking over as housekeeper here. If I have given satisfaction, that is to say," she added doubtfully.

"I shall tell her ladyship that I am quite satisfied with your work, Tory," Cressida said. "Such rampant loyalty as you have shown to the family should be rewarded. I'll make sure you will deal admirably with the Dowager Lady Dauntry — until we are ready for you to take over at the castle."

Tory's broad mouth split in a smile. "Now then, how about a nice cup of tea and a piece of my gingerbread that you are so fond of, your ladyship? I shall rouse Jennet up and tell her the good news. We will be merry as grigs, with the old malkin gone, taking her nasty nervous condition with her."

On this unservantlike speech, she left, and Cressida returned to her daydreams.

We hope you have enjoyed this Large Print book. Other Thorndike Press or Chivers Press Large Print books are available at your library or directly from the publishers.

For more information about current and upcoming titles, please call or write, without obligation, to:

Thorndike Press
P.O. Box 159
Thorndike, Maine 04986 USA
Tel. (800) 257-5157

OR

Chivers Press Limited
Windsor Bridge Road
Bath BA2 3AX
England
Tel. (0225) 335336

All our Large Print titles are designed for easy reading, and all our books are made to last.